PILGRIM'S HARBOR

PILGRIM'S HARBOR

Floyd Skloot

STORY LINE PRESS
1992

Copyright © 1992 by Floyd Skloot

First American Printing

All rights reserved. No part of this book may be reproduced in any form or by any electronic or mechanical means including information storage systems without permission in writing from the publisher, except by a reviewer.

This publication was made possible thanks in part to the generous support of the Andrew W. Mellon Foundation, and our individual contributors.

ISBN: 0-934257-71-X

Published by Story Line Press
Three Oaks Farm
Brownsville, OR
97327-9718

Book design by Lysa McDowell

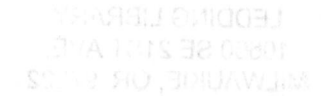

FOR BETSY

"... a company
Of sundry folk happening then to fall
In fellowship, and they were pilgrims all."

—Geoffrey Chaucer
The Canterbury Tales

CHAPTER ONE

I like excitement as much as the next guy. But the business here is repose.

Pilgrim's Harbor offers the atmosphere of a night in port, the illusion of haven, tranquility. It aspires to be mellow. I provide a place to park the car for the night free with the room, not home and never meant to be. My philosophy is let them rest, direct them to what they ask for, and turn the sign on early. The theme song would be a lullaby.

No one arrives here for the view, the ambience, the Big Time. My trade is succor, my currency is talk, and my client is the stranger.

***

Take last night and Gilbert Lucas. Or Lucas Gilbert. He didn't make that clear.

Filled in the register Gilbert Lucas, crossed it out, filled it in Lucas Gilbert. Then he put down cash and left without a signature.

We tried to talk while he was writing. He'd look up, the whites of his eyes saturated with a chestnut hue, and struggle to focus on my lips. He kept shaking his head clear like a boxer between rounds.

"Three states," he said. "I told my wife I'd drive three states on the 20th. But I forgot how big states are out here."

"You could be talking a lot of miles."

"912. No stops, either. Only for gas."

Lucas opened the door to leave, then stopped. One leg was in front of the other, mid-stride, but his left foot hadn't come all the way down to the floor. He sagged against the frame, frozen between collapse and revival.

I've seen the pose many times. He wasn't exactly falling.

"You need any help?"

"Not tonight. But if I'm going to be at the coast for the first day of summer, like I've been every year since 1951, I have to get up in two hours."

This guy doesn't want gambling night, a rec room, and a show in the lounge.

***

Pilgrim's Harbor is easy to find. When the road starts to shimmer, black as an ocean at night, look away from the setting sun and it's there. Exit, loop over the Interstate, and stay to the right.

It's along one of those stretches of road where drivers say it'll be better tomorrow, the worst is behind us. Unless they're going the other way, in which case it's let's rest up for tomorrow, we can do the whole thing in a day if we start early. Here, the formula is distance divided by speed equals tired, not time. Pilgrim's Harbor is for people going farther than one day will take them. My guests are the haggard drivers and the stiff passengers. They're journeyers heading to or from and hoping nothing will happen at Pilgrim's Harbor that will cause them to remember having stayed here.

Between turning on the Welcome sign and waiting

PILGRIM'S HARBOR 3

until No goes up beside Vacancy, I become part of the system. My smile and my wave are charged by the same current that charges the sign.

The Pruitt family bears full responsibility for the name Pilgrim's Harbor. It could be worse. Think of all the Chateaus and Beachcombers there are; the Caravans, Bel-Aires and Silver Fountains. Before the Pruitts bought it, the place was called the Klover Korner.

Jock Pruitt's a history buff and exploration was always his specialty. He taught fifth grade before striking oil right in the backyard. All his students loved the unit on explorers, especially at Thanksgiving, when he tied it in with the holiday.

"Pilgrim's Harbor" came to him in a dream the night he purchased it. Within a month, the Klover Korner Motel had a new name and image, though from time to time people still come in looking for rooms with waterbeds and mirrors and adult films.

We've got a detached restaurant called Harbor Side and a play room called The Pier. There's a gas station across the cloverleaf, another a half-mile beyond the motel, and no other place to eat except downtown.

The motel has 59 units. Color TV, air conditioning, three kitchenettes, a pool. Doors are painted alternating colors: orange, blue, brown; orange, blue, brown. Everything is screwed down tight—artwork, television, lamps—and a guest would have to be a genius to get one of the chairs out a door. It's all in good shape. New insulation, soundproof against the noises of normal neighbors, and extra towels at no cost.

I have a little room behind the office with a recliner and hide-a-bed, telephone, TV and stove, a steady walnut table, a few remnants for a rug. It's adequate for my needs.

If a guest looked over my office, he'd get a good idea of the mood around here. Open and hospitable, simple without being chintzy. He'd know he was in the west, but there wouldn't be chaps or saddles or Big Sky paintings.

***

She stood in the doorway a long time. Scandinavian, I could tell at a glance.

Tiina Andersson had the largest feet and hands I'd ever seen on a woman, the kind that could palm a steering wheel. She also had the narrowest shoulders.

The longer I looked—and I looked a long time because she just stood there—the odder her assembly seemed. The hips were so wide it didn't seem possible for her to come through the door without turning sideways. The hair was just long enough so it didn't stand up like a crew cut. She wore baggy corduroy slacks and a purple cotton sweater that gave no indication of contours beneath.

Yet the woman was beautiful. She walked, finally, with the slow grace of a Percheron.

"I have special needs," she said when I offered her the pen.

"Well, things are fairly standardized here. Like, all the beds are double."

"I don't sleep on a bed, I sleep on the floor. My cats sleep on the bed."

"Cats?" Ocelots, right? "Our policy is no pets in the rooms. People come through here with allergies, especially in the summer. I mean, they react no matter how thoroughly we clean the rooms."

"I could pay extra. Like for an extra person in the room."

"Couldn't they sleep in the car?"

"They could. But I couldn't. And I don't sleep without my cats."

She smiled, she didn't raise her voice, but Tiina Andersson sounded menacing. Her eyes flashed at me from beneath false lashes that were thick as spikes. I like to be flexible. Cats could be better than dogs in a motel room. So I smiled back at her. She blinked slowly and I wondered if she'd be able to open her laden eyes again.

"I suppose a couple of cats wouldn't be too bad," I said. "Maybe you could put an extra blanket on the bed, if you have one with you? Keep the cooties off our bedding."

"You're very kind." She began to fill out the registration card with a pen of her own. It had a calligraphic nib and she wrote slowly, with flourishes, talking in a clicking whisper. "I have to leave them alone all day when I go to the office, so I don't like to leave them when we're on vacation. Of course, it's more than a couple, but I would put blankets out even if you didn't ask me to. They couldn't sleep otherwise."

"More than a couple?"

"I left several with colleagues at home. I only brought six with me."

***

There are freeways in this country that run smooth to the visible horizon. These roads are part courtesy, like a calm sea, and part treachery, like sheer ice. But I can't tell that story. That story is what my guests can tell.

I see the sun and the poor choice of colors in this part of America. I feel the gusting wind and the thick humidity. But most of my time is spent inside. That's what stopped me before.

I'm getting too close to forty to keep putting important things off. Besides, this business is a gas, a trip, a slice o' life.

My name is Duane Howser. That was also my grandfather's name and my cousin's name. So people have always called me Dewey.

I'm thin. This is not due to regular exercise or careful diet, but to a squirrel-like metabolism. I move fast. In fact, I move so fast that it's important for me to have my work surroundings orderly so I won't knock into things like a blind man when I zip around the office. It's a struggle for me to appear relaxed when guests arrive and I've trained myself to be still when I talk to them. Jumpy hosts don't inspire confidence. I have the kind of hair that looks long even when it's cut short, a pouf of dark curls that are thick all the way to their ends. Before it mussed my hair, a wind would have to be fierce enough to blow the whole frizz right off.

My complexion, which at first glance seems tanned and healthy, is actually closer to khaki. I'll take khaki one step further and admit my skin seems subject to the random wrinkling that occurs to woolen uniforms.

In direct light, I look almost twice my age.

People think I slouch. But my posture is more like that of a person who has been punched hard in the solar plexus. If I could just catch my breath, you think, then I would stand up straight.

My lopsided smile and cinnamon colored eyes make strangers at ease with me. I cock my head sideways and listen to people with interest, always appearing on the verge of offering dinner. This, together with an uncanny short-term memory for detail, lets me converse with my guests and seem both familiar and informed.

CHAPTER TWO

A guest came in today at around 3:30. The maids were done, it was still getting warmer, and I was standing at the door watching the sun hit the quiet swimming pool surface.

3:30 is early for this time of year. Lots of daylight left. Usually a guy alone tries to drive until he's too exhausted to go on, then checks in and grumbles because the pool is in the shade or because it's too sunny by his room. *Right, I'll take care of it.*

He was from Rhode Island. Woonsocket. Which is still, I told him, a lot bigger than where he was staying this first night of summer.

I like talking to my guests about where they're from or where they're going. But it can be a tricky business.

Some people don't want to talk about their homes. They don't trust strangers, or maybe they're just superstitious. Like I'm going to sneak off in the night while they're asleep in #34 and raid their empty house halfway across the country. Or maybe call my New England connections and give them the address so they can send out a team.

Then there are others too tired or mean-spirited at the end of a day's travel. I can pick them out just from the way they ask about the rates, even though my sign is explicit, or the way they ask if the coffee in the rooms is any good. Who ever had good coffee dumped out of a little tinfoil packet into lukewarm water in a motel room?

I'm not knocking car travel. Motels would have no

part in the hospitality industry if they hadn't quit rationing gas after the war and let people drive all those cars. But it seems to be a bad way to go, judging from the way people stagger into Pilgrim's Harbor. So I've learned how to pick out a person who's willing to talk.

Woonsocket sure was. I wasn't at all surprised to learn his field was politics. But nice as he was to have around, I wish now he'd never come.

Politicians make terrific motel guests. Entertaining talkers, friendly to strangers, and, in a highway motel, off duty. If they're stopping at Pilgrim's Harbor, they aren't working any constituents, aren't dealing with things back in the district, aren't plying the trade.

Mr. Richard L. Finfer stopped early just so he could get off the road, start talking to somebody, and shake a hand. Judging from the condition of his suit and beard, he hadn't been with another human being in a couple of days. Cotton doesn't ride well in June, but Finfer looked handsome scruffy.

He was heading back home to help a woman run for Governor. Finfer grew up with her in Woonsocket, a town of about 50,000 where he said everybody who qualifies makes it a point to vote. Now he was going to move her to Providence.

"I like that slogan," I said.

"Plenty of time to do slogans this week."

"Beats listening to local radio stations, right?"

"Or learning Italian by tape."

"So you've been in campaigns before."

I'm a believer in turning questions into compliments. It's a good way to help business. But as I stood there nodding at him wisely, Finfer laughed. It was a quick exhale through his nose.

"Just classrooms. Berkeley. Ten long years teaching

Polly Sigh."

"Well, then you'll probably lend authority to her campaign."

"If she wasn't such a novice, she wouldn't have me." Finfer didn't seem to be in a rush to check in, but I strolled behind the counter and turned the registration card stack around toward him. Without stopping his conversation, Finfer took a sleek silver Parker out of his breast pocket and filled out a card.

"What do you get out of it?" I asked.

"Nothing. Summer work for my students, maybe a staff job for me if she wins. Head the State Board of Education. I'm not thinking that far down the road."

"She must be pretty, then. I bet that's worth votes."

"A bright woman. I was in love with her for twelve years. Then we graduated from high school and lost touch."

Finfer looked down at the registration card and frowned. He scratched out the address he'd written, then stared as if I were a student who couldn't understand a simple question.

"I'm between addresses," he said.

"Doesn't matter."

I don't care if the guest's address is in the records. But the man I work for does.

Every few years, the politicians try to make it a law. For the insurance lobby, for the law enforcement lobby, for the hotel/motel association. It makes me laugh. Like they'd know if an address some guest wrote down was false. But I try to make everybody comply, since there isn't much mileage in having Jock Pruitt upset with me.

"We've got a bunch of old friends all coming together to map out a strategy," Finfer said as if there'd been no confusion between sentences. He must be a great classroom talker. "Lots of people have the campaign itch, you know. Like to take a crack at this kind of thing. It's fun."

It was easy to like him. Standing with his elbow on the blotter, in his element, car door open, engine running and directional signal still blinking, Finfer didn't hurry away. He was my kind of guest. He checked out the tourist brochures, scanning the front page of *The Courier*, and didn't ask when the pool closed or the bars opened or when checkout time was.

His looks were the kind people call classy. Tall and lean, he had a graying walrus-moustache that distracted you from the weakness of his chin. He stood just a degree shy of erect, with his loosened tie tugged over so the knot was half-hidden by the point of his collar, and had a voice that was part hush and part song.

***

Why travel America when there's Richard Finfer right here? I knew him as well as any friend I had. But I never dreamed that he could change my life for good.

I knew he'd be back to spend time with me as soon as he'd settled into the room. I'd seen versions of Finfer before. These people zip all around the country between elections, landing here like leaves falling at the end of summer.

He pulled nose-first into the spot in front of #21, not needing to back in since there wasn't much to unload. The man was trying to make the continent in four or five days. For what? Get back home to Woonsocket and spend a couple of crazy months campaigning for some old girlfriend. Probably see cousins he hadn't seen in twenty years, maybe a brother, the parents' graves.

I could tell what Finfer's made of, could see it all over him, American as Pike's Peak (which I've heard is not such a great place to go). He's going to zoom from one end of his little state to the other, Sound to Massachusetts, staying in motels, and maybe once in a while in somebody's home at Kingston or Cranston, if his candidate looks like she might at least make it through the primary, and he's going to be so frazzled come November that he won't know where he's been or what to do next.

Finfer knows it. And I know he's happy.

But the guy is going to get up on some platform in a place like Central Falls or Warwick and words are going to rush out like a stream melting down in spring. This is a different kind of speaking than he'd do if he were from Manitou Springs, Colorado, or Fitzgerald, Georgia. It goes beyond accent and is something I've learned to hear when the words come out of my guests. Finfer will not be at home and will suffer.

I watched him lock his door and walk to the office. I went behind the counter so he wouldn't think he was being watched.

Finfer had changed into white sneakers and a zip-up blue sweater. When he opened the door gently, the bell merely tinged.

"Got the time?"

"Four ten. Forget to reset your watch, Mr. Finfer?"

"No. Forgot to wind it this morning."

"You ought to get one of those self-winding models. Shake hands and wind your watch at the same time."

Finfer was one of those people who makes you feel your idle conversation is of value to him. His expression offered deep appreciation. I'd solved a major problem and put Finfer in my debt. Maybe I could run the Rhode

Island Tourism Bureau if Finfer's candidate won.

"I'm supposed to call some people, let them know where I am. Now's as good a time as any."

"Why not do it from your room? We can settle up in the morning."

"Be gone too early. Besides, I like using pay phones." He handed me two dollars for change.

Finfer waved and walked toward The Harbor Side, pocketing the coins. I understood that if Finfer used the phone in his room, he'd have to talk standing up and find a place to rest his elbow, something to watch going past while he spoke.

One thing I learned long ago was that travelers are usually set in their ways. And people who are set in their ways are very difficult.

***

Caught up in doing a thing they like, all people are set in their ways. It follows that people pursuing their dreams are difficult because they're set in their ways.

When I lived in the midwest for a couple of years, taking courses at one after another of the state-supported schools around Chicago, I had a girlfriend who read both the *Tribune* and *Sun-Times* cover to cover every Sunday morning. This was her dream of leisure.

I couldn't talk with her at all during the process, except perhaps to ask if she wanted her coffee warmed. She would look at me when I started a sentence, smile as if she recognized me for an old pal, and if I went on to a second sentence her eyes would move down to the news again. She couldn't help it. Every ad, editorial, local obits, Feminique, even the box scores of the Seattle-Oakland game. She'd cut out features to pass on to friends; study the reviews of books, movies, albums, restaurants; scan the want ads and the lost and found; price dogs. Black hands at noon.

I'm the same way during my shift at Pilgrim's Harbor. I'd be difficult if anyone I knew from elsewhere showed up. In fact, I hardly know anyone from elsewhere. I prefer it that way.

How do people think about clothes or friends or groceries when they're working? Those things don't carry any weight when I'm dealing with the motel or my guests.

I figure that's the main reason I never got married. In fact, it's possible that I will never marry, at least not while I'm in the business. I want to be available to Pilgrim's Harbor, free to do what needs to be done when it needs doing. That isn't consistent with my idea of being married.

I would say I'm between girlfriends at present. It doesn't bother me, I get by all right, but I'm open if anything comes along.

***

I ought to say that I'm not a seasoned veteran with the women. Started late and progressed slowly.

Throughout the time I was growing up, we moved at least once every year. Sometimes several times a year. That's not the way to cultivate young love, I tell you.

I never got to know anybody very well. Just about the time I'd have a sweetheart targeted, it was time to relocate. There were several schools I went to where I never did get the names of the kids in my home room straight.

Like a ballplayer who gets traded from team to team,

I would often fail to catch the signs. It was easy to let people down that way.

With all the shifting around, you'd think I might become an expert at getting acquainted. I probably did—that would explain why being an innkeeper comes so easily—but without proceeding to the more advanced business of intimacy. Even though I tried to fit in, I had a greater knack for neutralizing people than for attracting them.

***

Since I was still a virgin at 21, I decided to buy myself the experience as a birthday gift. It was to be a simple transaction, but I wasn't sure where to go to make it.

After two nights of rambling around the bars, I was walking to the bus stop when a stunning, young black woman emerged from between two buildings. This was downtown Chicago, for God's sake, but I was beyond fear at that point.

She was thin and short, with a head of hair that was as dark as the night. It was hard to see just how much hair was up there.

"Hello, baby," she whispered. I was engulfed by an exotic smell, something sharp like ginger. "What's your name?"

"Bob," I said. "My name's Bob. Bob Johnson."

"We must be related." She looked up and down the street, which didn't make me feel very comfortable. "I'm a Johnson, too. Yvette, if you can believe that."

"I've never known an Yvette."

She took my arm, nudging me west.

"That's because it's not as common a name as yours,"

she said.

I looked down at her while we walked. "You're cute."

"So why don't we go have a little fun together?"

"I, uh, I'm not staying around here."

"I see." She stopped walking. "And where *are* you staying, Mr. Bob Johnson?"

"At home." I shrugged. "I took the train in."

"Shoot! Why you walking down here then?"

"Hoping I might find you, I guess."

"You put fifty dollars in your pocket, in case you did?"

"Fortunately."

So she walked me through an alley to an old motel. It was a terrifying place that smelled of melted plastic and was lit by bare, red bulbs. She engineered the acquisition of a room for a half-hour and led me upstairs. I don't think the door locked.

"You want it on or off?" she asked.

I had no idea what she was referring to. Her clothes? I thought clothes were a them, not an it.

"Off."

Then so quickly I wasn't sure it happened, she took off her hair. Beneath the wig, there was just a hint of her own close-cropped hair tied down with a gray net. I gaped.

Then she took off her coat, her high heeled shoes, her belt, and all her clothes with one shrug of a shoulder. I'd never seen a black woman naked before, not even in pictures.

She looked thirteen everywhere except her face.

She pointed at my crotch. "Let's have a look at Mr. Johnson."

I got the economy package. She was astonished by what I didn't understand.

"What do you like?" she asked.

"What can I have?"

There was a lot to accomplish in thirty minutes.

***

Between Yvette and now, I've been involved with three women seriously. There've also been a few more one nighters, all for free.

A year ago, there was a girl who worked in the Harbor Side. Nikki Snyder, local girl, a waitress, just out of high school.

Nikki had only a rough draft of eyebrows and long lashes that looked almost lavender in the sunlight. She was breast-bone high on me and eager as fireweed.

She didn't mind meeting only when the schedules permitted, didn't try to come up to the office, didn't try to get special privileges. We would take walks. I couldn't keep up with her and still breathe normally.

"You're an old man," she would tease.

"I'm not much past thirty."

"You could be 22 for all I care and you'd still be an old man."

Once I started getting into shape and we began to take longer walks, I realized we had no density together, nothing much to talk about. I had twelve years on her and Nikki didn't see innkeeping as a career path.

Still, I was upset when she took off with Rick Betts from the service station across the cloverleaf. He wasn't even a local.

It was nice while it lasted. Nikki would sometimes drive me out to the countryside in her '63 red Falcon, a box in terrible shape. She knew where the creeks were, the clearings in the woods, the old bridges. The trunk of her Falcon was equipped with a cooler, blankets and pillows, tubes of lotions and jars of oils.

"See that sign over there?" she would ask, speeding past a stop sign and putting my hand on her leg. "Well, don't believe everything you read."

She was right. I was too old for her and I would always be too old.

What a sophisticated kid, I thought the first time we went out. I hadn't tried outdoor sex before Nikki.

It was very uncomfortable to be naked in a meadow. There was something about actually having all the clothes off my body and not being inside some room that made me feel too exposed. She didn't seem bothered, though. Cavorted like a deer around the meadow where she'd spread the blanket, laughing at me with my pants down around my ankles.

It was about a month before I was able to strip completely. It was another month before I was relaxed enough to do some of the things she wanted me to do that took a long time. That was the only year I didn't mind early frost.

It's been a long time since Nikki. At my apartment, I've been carving a lot. Carving is something I learned as a boy in Tennessee or Kentucky, I forget which. I don't do my carving at Pilgrim's Harbor.

It's the kind of thing I do in spurts. Years can go by without my touching a knife, but then I'll have the urge to work on wood again and there it is. You don't forget.

My skills have developed to the point where I can do intricate figures, gnomes and old men with canes, a mother and baby. Last time I took up carving, I started out with little knife-like pieces, straight and easy enough, a few sharks, wolf, derringer.

But I've progressed far enough in the last year to make figures that stand, heads I can paint in detail, smooth things that feel good in the hand. Sometimes I think of putting the stuff out for an exhibit, to see if it would sell.

It's late. The only reason I'm talking about carving is because I was talking about women. Rather, about not having one right now.

From time to time, a woman will pull into Pilgrim's Harbor and put me in a difficult situation. Two or three times a year a man will approach to register and look at me with interest. Occupational hazards.

I'm always on the lookout for interesting encounters, but won't do anything to hurt business. I like quickies, the flyers. They're the safest.

My work keeps me from being lonely. It puts me face to face with people. I see them tired out first, but then I get to say good-bye when they're refreshed. I get to know what they want to let me know.

All things considered, what I have here is a good deal. I would be the first to admit that. It's certainly not my intention to complain.

CHAPTER THREE

Richard L. Finfer left before six a.m., having slipped the key through the mail slot. He also propped a half empty pint of J&B against the door.

It must have fallen inside gently enough not to break when Mike Strummer, the morning clerk, opened the door. He put it beside my desk.

Most guests would have poured the unfinished Scotch down a drain or taken it along with them. It was a nice thank you.

I held the thin green bottle to the afternoon light and sloshed the Scotch around. I found myself hoping Finfer would stop in again on his way back.

***

Returners aren't common at a highway motel. But some people have a regular route they use every year and they like to break their trips up the same way each time. Those who do return let me know if I forget they've been here before.

One family stopped twice a year ever since I began to work at Pilgrim's Harbor. The Ogdens, from Olympia. They come through in late spring, usually June, heading for their kids' homes in the Smokies, and then come through again in October heading back to Washington.

I thought about them because another couple from Olympia stayed at Pilgrim's Harbor last night. The man was Angus Petty and his wife was Christina. They play bridge with the Ogdens and came here at their recommendation.

I gave the Pettys their ice bucket and let them have four tea-bags free instead of charging them. It seemed like a good investment. Even gave them room #15, which is the Ogdens' favorite. Air conditioning works well and the beds are extra firm.

I wouldn't have guessed they'd be complainers. I also don't blame them.

A young guy checked in about 9:00 and took my last room. I'd been saving #16, hoping to let the Pettys be by themselves. But I had to give this N. Holmes a room.

N. Holmes was traveling with a girl who couldn't have been more than 18 years old, if that. They were carrying a baby in one of those Snugglies that look like an overstuffed backpack. It was N. Holmes' baby, I could see that clearly enough. Same wild red hair and pale skin, same big green eyes and mouth like a leaf from the Ficus tree, same huge rock of a nose. Signed up with Boise, Idaho, as his residence, but he had Iowa plates and a New England accent, so I couldn't be sure. But I didn't think N. Holmes was Idaho. No mountains in his eyes, no space in his voice.

Then I got a call at 9:10 from Angus Petty. There was too much noise from the next room.

"What kind of noise, Mr. Petty?"

"Arguing, throwing suitcases or something around hard, kid crying. Can you do something?"

"I don't think so. Not yet. If it persists, I'll call them and issue a complaint."

Although we were trying to be nice to each other, I could hear that Petty wanted me to put a stop to the noise right then. But since he was friends with the Ogdens, I guess Petty didn't want to make trouble at one of their favorite motels. Besides, he might have thought there were rules through the Innkeepers' Union that governed when I could meddle.

Asking people to quiet down is always touchy. If they were considerate people, they wouldn't be making the noise in the first place. I'm guaranteed to get abuse and little cooperation, but sometimes I have to do it.

At 9:40, Petty knocked at the office door. He was in his undershirt and pajama pants, wore open-backed brown vinyl slippers, and looked a little deep into his cocktails. But he was polite.

"I'm afraid I must insist that you intervene in Room 16."

"Still at it?"

"Young man, it's both very loud and very off-color. My wife. I must insist."

I hesitated. Physical confrontation is not something I'm good at. But my voice is firm and deep, a good instrument, full of a confidence I don't always feel. Remember the voice, I told myself.

First, I called N. Holmes on the phone rather than dealing face to face. He didn't answer. So much for the disembodied voice approach.

"Maybe he's gone out to cool off," I said.

"I didn't see him leave. He must know that any calls would be in complaint and so he ignored it. I will accompany you if you wish, but I do insist."

It sure seemed like a long hike down to the room. Petty and I walked single-file and tip-toe, two experienced guerrilla warriors on patrol.

N. Holmes seemed to have expanded a fourth again his size. He was as red as a circus balloon and seemed ready to burst. He yanked the door open, looked me and Petty over, and inhaled hugely.

"Buzz off."

He slammed the door. I heard his little companion screech and close what sounded like a closet door.

I could imagine what the interior must look like. Alla Mae was going to be furious in the morning when she got to #16.

I knocked sharply, motioning Petty to the side in case N. Holmes became violent. Things were escalating pretty fast in the room. Petty stood his ground.

"Mr. Holmes, I will have to call the police if you

continue to disturb other guests."

There was no response. Of course, I realized, N. Holmes had ended up in a room with an orange door. Fellow held onto a rage very well.

From there, it got to be a very bad night. N. Holmes' activity soon took a different form. He began calling me to complain about Petty's television being too loud. Petty said he was only trying to drown out the racket from N. Holmes. Then N. Holmes asked for an additional set of towels. Said he'd had to use theirs to stuff under the locked door between his room and Petty's because of the cigarette smoke. Petty complained about the smell because N. Holmes had apparently wet down the towels with ammonia. On and on.

Things got more tense all night, through me, until finally I had to summon Delbert Simmons to deal with N. Holmes. I've only called the police three times since starting at Pilgrim's Harbor. But this one was beyond me. I was sorry for the Pettys' bad luck.

***

I remember this fight I was in once as a kid. My forté was speed, as in running away, but this fight happened so fast there wasn't time to flee.

Seymour "Fist" Hesser ruled the afternoon schoolyard when I was twelve and living on Long Island. That was fine with me, since I always left the school grounds immediately after the bell rang.

This one afternoon Fist was conducting a curve-ball clinic. A group of disciples had already formed near the schoolyard exit and Fist was throwing a rubber ball against the school's wall. There was a box chalked on the wall, with an X inside it, and Fist was making his curves hit where the X crossed. He must have been a good pitcher, now that I think of it. Everyone was smiling and no one was asking to try a pitch himself.

My mistake was walking between Fist and the wall while he was lining up his next pitch. I happened to think that was the most sensible time to cross the line and make it out of the yard unscathed.

"Hey, Howser, you fucked up my concentration."

"Sorry, Fist," I mumbled. Then I turned and walked back to where I'd begun crossing his line of fire. "I'll wait till after you pitch."

"Come over here. I want to talk to you."

Those were still my gullible years. I went over, a smile on my face, and walked into Fist's left hook.

Apparently, I was lucky he had the ball in his right hand. I remember very little except the bizarre sense of warmth inside my head and the way my fingertips tingled. It also seemed astonishing to me that a punch could actually make you fall down, like in the movies.

I was up and running almost before I hit the ground. There was laughter and some shouted words that sounded threatening but have faded from memory.

My experience with Fist exhausted my interest in fighting. I've found that this lack of interest extends to verbal fighting as well, although I can't hang that on Fist Hesser. Still, I don't like open conflict of any kind and tend to retreat from argument as I retreated from fisticuffs.

This would be another reason my choice of career makes sense. You hardly get to know anybody well enough here to fight with them. Especially if the product is satisfactory, which I make sure mine is.

Then again, there are always the N. Holmeses.

CHAPTER FOUR

A man came in around 6:00 and all I could see was Horse. He asked for the end room in order to park his U-Haul where he wouldn't be surrounded.

He was from DuBois, Wyoming, and he worked the tourist season giving hour-long rides on horseback. Took people up a steep, rocky hill and let them gallop along the top of the butte a while, sit and soak up the view, snap a few photos. Then he walked them down.

Charged $8 per person and took eight or ten at a time. An easy $90 an hour with tips, in season, and more if he wanted to.

He did his vacation traveling early, so he could be in DuBois for the summer traffic. I thought I knew what was in the trailer.

He must be tough on his horses. He was the sort of fat that gets organized from neck to waist—reedy legs, long neck below a softball sized head, straw for eyebrows, nose like a saddlehorn. I'll remember his boots for a long time, three colors up the side and thick four-inch heels with stars on them. They fit like hooves.

***

In the dark hallway of the Harbor Side, where the pay phones line the corridor to the restrooms, the Horseman found Finfer's briefcase. He brought it up to the office and helped me go through it.

I wish now that I'd thrown the thing away. I wish I'd turned it over to Delbert Simmons and been done with it.

The briefcase seemed more like a valise than a portable document carrier. It wasn't the sleek sort of item that a businessman normally carries, with the little compartments and the secret-code locks, but it also wasn't the kind you could drop out of a helicopter without damage.

What we had in our hands was the man's soul. A good quantity of his earthly possessions too.

Obviously, Finfer hadn't mastered computers. It was going to be an old-fashioned campaign.

There were legal tablets—yellow ones, white ones, several with a greenish tint—lined and unlined index cards the same colors as the tablets, pens and markers, expandable folders stuffed with papers, photocopied articles from magazines, a book on public finance in the fifty states, pages and pages of names, addresses and prices. The loaded briefcase weighed almost sixty pounds.

There were a lot of half-finished things scattered inside. Speeches, reports, letters. I had no idea briefcases could hold so much.

But there was no address. It looked like Finfer had thrown away the California identification tags and not yet replaced them with the Rhode Island.

I've tracked down people before. I knew I could call City Hall in Woonsocket for a start and see if they knew the name of a woman running for Governor. I could get in touch with almost anybody if I had to.

I felt I had to.

There were items in the briefcase that Finfer would want right away. The thing would cost a fortune to mail, unless he was willing to wait three weeks to get it parcel post. Maybe Finfer would call me first.

He sure has messy penmanship. It's a real jerky writing with long ripples and waves where you'd think letters ought to be. I might not have been able to decipher an address even if one was available. Would sure hate to be Finfer's secretary when he's heading the Rhode Island Board of Education.

***

After we'd gone through the briefcase, the Horseman cocked his hat back and looked around like a cowboy checking over the range. He let out a little snort and I thought I heard leather creak when the man shifted his weight. He spoke with a surprisingly high voice.

"Seen guys like that before. They come to ride a horse, tell me about how they used to ride all the time when they were kids back east." He shook his head. "Then they go off and forget their shoes or something."

It was strange to have a person at Pilgrim's Harbor who knew some of the things I know about travelers. But the Horseman hadn't studied them with any sympathy.

"I like those clowns who sit up there in the saddle and make lots of clicking noises. They rock back and forth and whoop trying to get a horse to start walking. Seen guys bunch up the reins and whap the horse a couple swats on her neck, flail away with their tennis sneakers. Don't know what the hell they're doing, but they sit there telling me they've had 46 years of lessons."

"How do you keep from laughing?"

"One way is it ain't funny." The Horseman wasn't smiling. "I'm waiting for some guy to try mounting with a running leap onto some old mare's back. End up with a new asshole. They've seen too many movies is what it is."

"A person can seem pretty foolish, out of his element," I said. What I really wanted to say was *Hey, easy on them, they're only your livelihood.*

"Too hammerheaded to pour piss out of a boot."

I stared at him. Here was a guy who made a life out of serving people he didn't like. He seemed like the kind who grew meaner and more bitter the happier and more relaxed he felt.

"Anybody ever get hurt on you?"

"Kind of shape most people are in, they get hurt just trying to raise a foot into a stirrup. Couple guys fall off, not too many, and a couple kids get scared. It's about as dangerous as picking potatoes."

***

DuBois, Wyoming. No Holiday Inn in DuBois. The nearest one is over in Thermopolis, where the hot springs bring in some tourists. None of the chains has a set-up in DuBois.

Elk and deer hunting, good Wind River trout, and located on the only road from Casper to Yellowstone. No chains, but there are places like Pilgrim's Harbor in DuBois.

The Branding Iron, Red Rock, Sage, and Twin Pines. A place to eat good Wyoming beef down the main street and a couple of ranches. Whenever there's a bad fire up on Whiskey Mountain, the steak place is closed to tourists and they feed the firefighters in shifts.

I like to size up places I hear about from guests, figure out prospects for the kind of motel I want to own someday. I'm not sure I want to stay at Pilgrim's Harbor the rest of my life, but I do think I want to maintain this way of life.

Not in Wyoming, though. I'm all for space, but a person has to have the prospect of traffic, has to fill the units regularly. Wyoming, especially up north there, was just not on the way to enough places. It was just 356 miles worth of a bad day's driving.

I suspect these thoughts are useless anyway. With what I've saved, I'd be hard pressed to own a bungalow.

***

I watched the Horseman sashay toward the Harbor Side. It bothers me when I'm glad to see a person leave. That was the case with this guy, even though he was only being friendly.

He seemed to raise little puffs of dust with every step, though the walk was paved between the motel and restaurant.

Suddenly, a young woman in jeans and a halter tied up to show most of her midsection materialized right out of the Horseman's image. She walked casually toward the office.

I stared. One moment I was watching the Horseman walk away, I blinked, and then this sweet figure with legs four and a half feet long, a naked middle, and a flimsy rag on top was walking toward me.

She must have belonged with the Datsun Z in front of the Harbor Side. I hoped she was going to check in rather than just ask the time, or how far it was to the border, or whether I had change for a five.

I backed away to get behind the counter, knowing I'd have to get hold of myself. It was just the surprise of the way I'd first seen her. I make it a rule to avoid flirting with the guests.

But this doesn't mean that I don't enjoy it when a young woman traveling alone stops in for the night. Spices things up, at least in my imagination, turning a

bowl-of-broth night into three-alarm chili.
I'm no hustler. It's bad business to trifle with a guest. But sometimes they come in friendly and I'd say I like to fantasize.

I certainly wasn't going to rule anything out altogether. There were too many things in life that had different meanings depending on who initiated them.

Crissy Chrysler was from Springfield, Illinois. She stayed in my office after checking in and asked if it was too late to swim.

"You've got till ten."

"I can't rest at all on a summer night until I've had my swim."

She had a cornfield of a smile and very long black hair. Three times since she walked in, she had me mesmerized while she reached back and grabbed the whole fall of hair, lifted it slowly to cool her neck, closed her eyes and wiggled her head around.

It was very confusing because there was so much to watch. The eyes rolled shut slowly, the gentle round face took on an expression of rapture, and there was all that movement inside the halter. I settled on watching the legs. I couldn't help seeing their languorous power. Ms. Chrysler was quite an act.

"Land of Lincoln, huh?"

I had to say something. The staring was making me uncomfortable, though it didn't seem to faze her.

"It's enough to drive you batty," she whispered.

Planted firmly, slightly parted, the legs were still while she kept everything above them going. It was like watching a child's mobile wind down and I began to hear familiar music played too slow.

"I like Franklin Pierce, myself," is what I managed to say.

"We've got Lincoln's law offices restored, his tomb, the house he owned, the depot where he left for Washington and where the casket came back. Big chunk of the town's still in 1848. Abe's Cafe, Abe's Amble, Lincoln Inn." A little bump and grind accompanied each item.

"Big attraction."

"Every bench downtown has something he said etched on it. A person hesitates to rest her buns on that sort of thing."

"I'll bet you had to study Lincoln all during February when you were in sixth grade, right?"

"Yeah," she opened her eyes wide and chuckled at me. "And seventh through tenth. 'Abraham Lincoln, the sixteenth president, born February 12, 1809, in a log cabin on Sinking Spring Farm. The only house he ever owned was at 430 South Eighth Street, right here in Springfield.' I'd swear there are 69 statues of him all over the city."

She inhaled for what seemed to be twenty seconds. I tried to think of something equally rich in innuendo. Nothing came to mind.

"That's pretty flat country," I said. Then, "Damn. I mean there isn't much relief." Then, "On the map."

"And hot, this time of year. Humid and hot."

She hit her consonants extra hard and seemed to be losing concentration. She looked out the window.

I was losing her. We'd been on Lincoln, topography, and climate too long. And I was definitely out of both practice and my element.

"Tell me, Ms. Chrysler, are you going to or from?" Maybe I could find out her plans.

Since she'd been in the one spot so long, just moving from the hips up, I wasn't prepared for her quick jump to my desk. I may have jerked back a little; I admit I lost my composure completely.

She leaned over and picked up the nameplate from my counter. She slid the plate out of its holder, turned my name upside-down, put it back in, and set it on the counter again. The whole maneuver took five seconds.

"What did you do that for?"

"Don't know. Thought you'd look cute if I got you flustered. I did and you do."

"Flustered is cute?"

"I like to keep my men off balance."

I couldn't decide whether to count 'cute' more than 'my men.' Maybe I brought it all on myself by asking a personal question.

She leaned over onto the counter and her legs were hidden from view. I must have been getting cuter, because what I could see was certainly keeping me flustered.

And, unfortunately, not adequately witty. She seemed to want repartee and I was gawking at her cleavage. Off balance indeed.

"Will you help me up if I fall?" I asked.

"What kind of name is Dewey, anyway?"

I could have answered straight and told her it was short for Duane, which was Celtic for "Poet." I could have played with her and said it was a poetic name, or said it was how I got when I saw women who looked like she did. Could could.

What I did say lacked a little in inspiration. It seemed to cost me.

"It's just a name."

A glaze came over her eyes. I've seen the same look come over some mothers when their child begins to tell me the story they'd all been listening to for six hours in the car. It's the Nth degree boredom look, almost embarrassment on your behalf.

I wasn't going to be worth the effort. She straightened up and all the languor was gone from her movements.

"Key please."

"Enjoy your stay."

She nodded, picked up her key, and left. She didn't return until much later and by then she was with the pop-eyed South Dakotan from Room #3. I'd put them far apart, but they met by the pool.

Good sport that I am, I gave them directions to "a nice restaurant, not the one here." Rick Baldwin, out of Sioux Falls. He already had an arm around her waist.

They came back around 11:00. I was watching TV, but I saw them. Went right to #3, came out immediately. Baldwin had a bottle in a sack.

Too bad he prepaid his room. Price for a double split between them would have been $14.25 each. This way, they had to spend $26 plus tax for their singles.

I have no right to complain.

CHAPTER FIVE

I got to work today glum. Sometimes, for all its variety and daily novelty, there are patterns here I've seen before.

It's like one of my mother's old quilts, with the eight designs dispersed throughout. I'd be lying on my side looking at the harsh octagon filled with teardrops, then turn to the other side and come smack up against another octagon instead of the friendly square filled with smiles that I was hoping for.

Or maybe it's just that I've seen myself blow it with

females before just like I blew it with Crissy Chrysler last night. Many times.

When I was a kid—this would have to be Lynchburg. No, couldn't be, I was too young. Has to be Lancaster. No, that even was before Lynchburg. Let's see: Seventh grade. So we're talking Cedar Rapids.

When I was in seventh grade, in Iowa, I sat behind this adorable, squeaky voiced girl named Jacqueline. Jackie, they called her, though I didn't have the nerve to call her anything except Hey. I did the same stunt with her that I did with Crissy Chrysler. I found myself unable to use the right kind of language, unable to talk to her except in ways that made her turn back around and face the teacher.

All this morning, I kept going over it. I kept trying to figure out what to do when it's time to acquaint. Maybe I ought to read more novels.

***

Also all morning, I made resolutions. I resolved to start exercising to stay sharp. I resolved to begin saving some cash every month. But the one that reaches vow level is that a number of things are going to have to change around here. Chief among them is the attitude of the maids.

Especially during this part of the year, the Pruitts want me to keep six maids full time and a flock of part timers. But the talent pool's pretty shallow. I get mostly kids from around the county doing summer work and a few older women, like Alla Mae, set in their ways.

Turnover is a big problem at Pilgrim's Harbor. The help doesn't pay attention to the proper way of making a bed, the one-trip-around method. Time's lost, blankets don't get spread to within eight inches of the headboard like they're supposed to be, corners aren't mitered, and the spreads look like hand-me-down shoes. The girls are always too tired to comply with the 2:00 deadline I set for their tasks.

One of the summer kids, Jennifer Pumphrey, can't be trusted making up occupied rooms. She won't take anything and Pilgrim's Harbor doesn't get many guests who stay more than one night, although sometimes during County Fair or Founders Week it happens, but she can't keep her hands off their belongings.

She fondles things and shifts them from desk top to dresser, table to ledge. She opens drawers, moves wallets and car keys, puts papers and magazines in odd piles, throws out stockings or bathing suits wrapped in towels. The sorts of things people notice.

The problem is that the kid generates complaints. This is particularly troubling since the mailing address for complaints is the Pruitts' home and Jock, the former teacher and historian, takes what people say in writing seriously.

As if her hot hands weren't enough, now the Pumph has all the other kids asking for extra pay if they work the Fourth of July weekend. She thinks it might be nice to celebrate the holiday away from home, to visit her boyfriend in the next county. So she invites her pals and would leave me with a workforce of two for the biggest weekend of the season.

"That's great," I told her. "Maybe I'll give discounts to any guests willing to make up their own rooms."

"But Dewey, we got a big party organized."

"What am I supposed to do, give Alla Mae some speed and pay her time-and-a-half? Here's a couple

Black Beauties, old timer, now go out there and clean."
"I'll find a few kids to fill in. How's that?"
"Just ducky. It took a month for me to train you. One of them cuts her carotid artery with a busted water glass and my liability insurance goes up 50%."
Then she showed her true colors. She looked down, slowly closed her eyes, and whispered as though afraid of being overheard.
"How about if only I go? I can uninvite the others."
I wasn't surprised. At her age, loyalty is as hard to hold onto under stress as virginity.
"Why didn't you come in and ask for the day off instead of stirring everybody up?"
When the Pumph starts to cry, she doesn't do it with the quivering chin or the welling eyes. No preliminary sobs or reddening of the nose tip. One second she's talking, the next she's in deluge, a grief-stricken widow in her third day of lamentation. She puts her hands to her ears so she can't hear what you say.
I patted her back. Faster than she had turned against her fellow vacationers, here I was saying "now now."
So it looks like I'll be one short for the Fourth and pay as if I had nine. But I also have something up my sleeve, another resolution. They're going to earn their extra.

***

Another thing that's going to have to change is the landscaping. It's bothering me. I resolved to talk to the Pruitts about it.
Pilgrim's Harbor relies on tulips—Golden Age, Bleu Aimable, Queen of the Night. They're up and gone inside of a month. Gladiolus, elegans, poppies. By late

May, well before the travel season begins in earnest, all the colors in front of the place are gone. I don't make policy and I'm not ready to plant my own, but the bare front during peak season is depressing. And another thing: the Pier needs one of those talking pinball machines. I first saw one at the Westview Center Shopping Mall, in the Fun Zone at the lower level. I put in my quarters and the thing started flashing like an ambulance, drums started pounding like a heart, and a voice grunted with fury ME HEKNAR! ME BEAT YOU!! Every bumper and knob made Heknar talk and the guy was no softie. It had more noise and lights than action, and it took 650,000 points to win a free game, but since Heknar had been in the Fun Zone I never saw anyone leave unhappy. All we have in the Pier is a couple of ding-dong type games, Sea Cruise and Camino Real, and one baseball game where the curveball never breaks and the fastball is too fast for the bat switch. There's also a computer quiz nobody plays, two foosball games, and a target game that hasn't been plugged in since I've been working here. People don't want to shoot at targets after a day aiming down the road. There's a pool table, but after three covers got ripped and all the balls swiped twice, I took it out.

Heknar's the answer. When the addicts come through, they always run up to the office in a frenzy. No pac man games or tank, no invaders. I send them out to the Mall. But maybe N. Holmes would have been less trouble if he could have worked out his aggressions on the machine.

***

The last resolution, the last change that absolutely has to be made, is in my luck. I don't mean only with the women, either. I need new luck with the overall guest situation.

There've been too many unpleasant ones lately. I wonder if it means something significant is happening to the whole country. I've been seeing more people who aren't enjoying their own leisure, aren't accepting the hospitality they're paying for.

Twice this season I've actually had folks check back out after looking over the room. I offered other rooms, offered to clear up any problems they could show me, but no—they had to leave.

Of course, right away I went to the rooms they were in and it was clear that nothing was wrong. I plopped on the bed, checked the tv and shower, looked for the Bible and the phone book. Everything right where it was supposed to be.

I had a lady come up to the office a week ago and throw a wet cake of soap at me. My reflexes aren't fast, but luckily her aim wasn't much either. Betty Wingate, from Cleveland. What's her problem? Nobody uses Ivory soap anymore and she wasn't about to herself. Dial, or at worst Camay.

One guy went out to check his car before turning in for the night and found a flat at the left rear. Does he change it? Does he politely come up here and ask me if I can help him change it? Hardly. Mr. Henry E. Laird, from Carson City, Nevada, calls me up and demands that I change his flat for him. Hangs up before I can explain that he at least has to wait until the motel fills for the night.

I could, unfortunately, go on and on. But that might give the false impression that I don't find this job satisfying.

I do. Said that a couple of days ago. It's just that, as of late, there sure are a lot of jerks on the highway.

CHAPTER SIX

Last night, before he went to bed, the Horseman came back up to the office. Made the trek especially to tell me he'd been thinking about Finfer's briefcase. He seemed angry.

"Your guy's probably going to want that case of his in a bad way."

"You're right. There's a lot of important work in it."

"Work, hell. That roster of names and numbers has to be their list of campaign contributors. Your friend's got to produce the list. Mister, politics begins and ends with cash."

"It shouldn't be hard to track him down. I can mail it to him right away."

"These guys don't believe in mail. The goddamn postmaster's a politician too, so they don't trust him much."

Not only did this make sense, it caused me to worry about having the briefcase around here. Security isn't something I know much about.

So this afternoon, I reached a cousin of Finfer's in Woonsocket. Four calls were all it took.

Area Code 401 Directory Assistance had no Finfers listed for Woonsocket, but City Hall told me the woman running for Governor was Elizabeth Mack Cowley. Her husband Willis told me she was in Pawtucket at a Rotary dinner and a ballgame, but first I had to promise I wasn't from the press.

"Finfer? Dick Finfer? Sure I know him," Willis Cowley laughed. "Had a crush on my wife all through school."

"I have something of his."

"So do I."

Cowley sounded sloshed. I tried to picture him tilted back in a recliner, watching the news, hoping he wouldn't have to see his wife singing "America the Beautiful" with the Rotarians and posing with the chapter president. His could be a difficult life.

"I think this stuff he left relates to the campaign," I said.

"Yeah, Beth said Finfer was coming back to help. It'll be good to see him."

"Well, I have his briefcase here. Should I send it to you? It seems to have important documents."

"No. God, no." Cowley snorted. I heard the clink of ice. "It's probably got all kinds of information we shouldn't have in the house." He stopped for a hacking cough, then added, "Send it to his sister, that'd be the ticket."

Cowley was ready to hang up. He gave me the sister's number and seemed to begin snoring.

"Goodbye. Thanks." I whispered, startling Cowley awake.

"But call her before you send the thing. Otherwise she'll just chuck it."

Margery Finfer Suttle was unaware that her brother would be coming to Woonsocket. Apparently, they were not often in touch. She sounded the way I thought Abigail Adams might sound. Her voice made my ear cold.

"Do not send it until Richard has arrived."

"I'll keep it as safe as I can in the office. It's not exactly a vault, though."

"Do keep it, dear fellow. I shall have Richard ring you up. It remains to be seen how he wishes to dispose of the item you possess."

But she hadn't sounded this way at first. At first,

she sounded frightened and confused. I felt as if I'd stumbled into Mrs. Finfer Suttle's bedroom and caught her without makeup or corsets, hair in curlers and a Vantage dangling from her pale lips. This wasn't shaping up as a good day. The call had a further depressing effect on me.

"Are you Richard Finfer's sister?" I had asked.

"Oh dear, has Richard harmed himself?"

"Is this his sister?"

"Oh, he's done it!"

"I'm calling because I'm a motel manager," I said with some confusion.

"Oh, it's sordid!"

"No, please." I'm never comfortable talking on the phone and have developed all sorts of tics that reflect my distress. I switched the receiver to the other side of my jaw. "I run a motel called Pilgrim's Harbor. A Mr. Richard L. Finfer of Woonsocket stayed here the night of June 21. When he left, he forgot his briefcase."

I spoke slowly and loudly, like people do when they talk to a foreigner. I seldom speak long-distance and was trying to cut through Mrs. Finfer Suttle's mounting hysteria. Unfortunately, I must have come across like Jack Webb. *Just the facts, ma'am.*

"Is Dickie all right?"

"Was when he left here, Mrs. Suttle."

"Has he been identified?" That one threw me. I wished I had a cup of coffee.

"Nothing's wrong, Mrs. Suttle. It's just that he left something behind here and I tracked him down to you. He told me he was heading for Woonsocket."

There was a long pause, as if she were playing back a tape of what I said. The only sound was a whiny sort of breathing which I was not inclined to interrupt.

"Oh good, I haven't seen him in years. He's so forgetful. Now what is it that you have of Richard's?"

"His briefcase. It's full of things he may need for the campaign."

"Campaign?" she asked, beginning to gain composure. "Not one of those at-large charities again I hope. The YMCA, or that hateful group who won't admit Jews?"

"He said he was coming home to help some woman he knows, Elizabeth Mack Cowley, run for governor."

"Bethie is seeking the governorship? How quaint."

"He said."

"And you have materials pertaining to this?"

"His briefcase. He left it when he checked out."

"Do not send it until Richard has arrived."

After hanging up, I thought about having Mrs. Finfer Suttle stay at Pilgrim's Harbor. She'd be the kind of solitary traveler I'd give #23 to.

I could see her coming in, dressed in a long-sleeved pale green dress with a buttoned collar in deepest summer. There was a hint of perspiration on her upper lip, a filigree of hair errant on her high brow. She asked for a single room, very clean, with an extra set of towels.

This wasn't what depressed me. It's that I once had a suicide at Pilgrim's Harbor, a man I'm convinced drowned himself in the pool. Mrs. Finfer Suttle's reaction to a stranger's voice asking if she was Richard Finfer's sister, her quick assumption that he'd harmed himself, brought the horrible afternoon back clearly.

***

Three summers before, just about the time I considered the motel finished with yesterday and ready for today, an enormous man drove up in a black Oldsmobile. He slammed it into Park so fast it rocked back and forth like a yacht through waves.

His name was Francis O'Banion. He was a good 6'5", with a nose that had often been broken and had sunk beneath the softest blue eyes, wore a white shirt unbuttoned to his breastbone and walked with a limp. His hands were perpetually clenched and looked like mallets.

If he's not in construction, I thought, then I'm not in hospitality.

The limp was from a prosthesis at the thigh. I found that out when O'Banion had on his bathing suit. His biceps were about twice the size of my neck.

O'Banion started drinking vodka straight from the bottle ten minutes after he had checked in and changed. He was stumbling around the pool, friendly enough and gregarious, waving at everyone. But he didn't ever smile.

The more he drank, the quieter he became. He got pale instead of red, didn't say anything unpleasant, didn't litter with the empty bottles. A couple of times, I saw him stand, reach out, and in pantomime seem to heave someone into the water.

After everyone left the pool area to change for dinner, O'Banion apparently took off his trunks and hung them on the branch of a fir near the pool. Then he must have taken off his prosthesis and flung it into the water.

About 8:00, a kid came running into the office screaming. I knew what it was even before he got the words straight.

There was a dandy investigation. Delbert Simmons came out in his black and white asking all sorts of questions, impounding O'Banion's Oldsmobile, taking his clothes and toilet kit, calling the relatives in New Jersey.

Delbert stood in the office with me, a 7x5 pad open in his palm, gathering background. The situation was obviously beyond both of us.

"Did he exhibit any unusual behavior?"

"Yes, officer. He killed himself."

"Come on, Dewey. Did he act strange?"

"Not too. Just checked in and drank two fifths of vodka in the hot sun. Nothing I would single out."

Delbert wrote *vodka* in his notes. He licked the pencil tip and wrote *sun*.

Unlike most gut-heavy men, Delbert didn't make a habit of hiking his pants up by the belt to rest a while on his stomach. He let the pants go and, instead, sucked his belly in and bowed down as if trying to push it all in under the belt. He did that a few times while analyzing his findings.

"Irish guy drinking vodka. Wouldn't you say that's strange, my man?" He looked at me with no expectation of an answer and wrote *strange* beneath *vodka*. "Did he leave a note?"

"You're the one who checked."

"Did he seem morose?"

"Delbert, stop it. I talked to the guy for as long as it takes to fill out a card."

"Maybe it wasn't suicide." Delbert took off his Seattle Mariners baseball cap, souvenir of last spring's trip out to see his sister. He adjusted the band in back, making it a notch smaller as if all this thinking had taken its toll on his hat size. "Drunk, fell in after his leg, died."

"Why'd he take off his leg?"

"Maybe it got uncomfortable, all that heat."

I waved my hand toward the pool. "Nobody saw it, so I suppose anything could have happened."

"In law enforcement, Dewey, nothing happens unless it's seen." He looked out toward the pool. "Insurance people too, they don't like assuming."

Delbert had huge ears, 80% lobe. But one look at his hard hazel eyes, forever shot with red, and you knew he was clever. He made people feel safe.

"What are you saying?" I asked.

"This here *mise en scène* is what we have to go by, that's all: Drunk, leg in pool, corpus in pool. Hell, we don't know if he fell in because his leg popped off from all the vodka, or what. Took it off in the water so he could climb out. Etcetera. You get it?"

"Hey, I'm not liable for a guy's suicide, am I? There wasn't any negligence, Delbert, I couldn't stop the guy."

"Easy. All I'm telling you is what we say makes a difference to the heirs, the insurance, the priest. Got to be careful, that's all. Damn, I have to get suspenders."

That was how the episode ended. But I had never seen behavior like O'Banion's before and I knew it had to be suicide.

Talking with Mrs. Finfer Suttle, I kept wondering how she could see any O'Banion in her brother. I supposed a person could do about anything if he's upset enough. But surely a lost briefcase wouldn't be grounds for him to snap. I hope Finfer calls somebody.

CHAPTER SEVEN

Just because you like to be with people doesn't mean you'd be a good innkeeper. You need to maintain an

edge.
There's skill in knowing which attributes of friendliness have to be exaggerated. If I were carving a statue of The Innkeeper, I'd have his face be all ear and mouth, with very little eyes and a teeny nose. You want to listen, talk only as much as it takes to keep the guests talking, and see/smell as little as possible.

But what you see you have to see keenly. Most people you don't have to keep watch on while they're staying overnight, so you can just listen and talk. But some bear scrutiny.

Probably the hardest thing to learn is that even though people seem to like you, seem to consider you a friend, it's fleeting. It's over in the morning.

***

A guest came in from Spokane, Washington. First thing he asked was whether I knew about the carousel.

I've had guests from Spokane before. I knew the name meant "Children of the Sun," I knew about EXPO 74, and I knew about the carousel. Now I know more.

Spokane has this downtown carousel designed as a present for a proud father's daughter. Handcarved, worth three million back when he drew it up, fastest carousel in the world.

It wasn't simply a carnival ride with the golden rings plucked for a free turn. It was semi-enclosed; each horse was different in shape, size, and color; and the rides were a long, smooth gallop.

The man who checked in was the nephew of the woman it was built for. To him, the carousel wasn't just a curio, or an object worthy of inclusion with the city tour.

It represented the depth of family love, the tradition of giving those you adore something lasting, the connection between romance and commerce.

I put this Anthony Sanderson in #21, the same room the Horseman from Wyoming had. Call it an experiment. Anybody who doesn't think guests leave a little something of themselves behind, even after the maids have been through, just doesn't understand the chemistry of the trade.

Sanderson was back in ten minutes asking for a different room. Said he never did that sort of thing, always kept his rare steaks even though he liked them well done, always tried to stretch the shoes that pinched his corns rather than complain about them. But there was something wrong with his room, wrong enough so he knew he'd never be able to sleep in it. Maybe he didn't like end rooms, he thought. He wanted to move and was very apologetic.

I felt guilty for playing with him. Sanderson had to pack up again and move a couple rooms over.

For penance, I put him in #27. The tv works well, with crisp colors, clear sound and reception on all three channels, and the shower is as sensitive as a hound's nose.

Sanderson's reaction to the first room made sense. Flesh horse didn't do for him what wood horse did and I could appreciate that.

Sent him a bottle of Burgundy, compliments of the house, and told him it was for the inconvenience. Our fault, not yours. Sanderson seemed pleased.

When it was all settled, Sanderson began to rise onto his toes and sink back down onto his heels. It was a peculiar movement of comfort, a kind of body-nod. I've seen people do odder ones and wouldn't have been surprised to hear a calliope.

***

I walked into my apartment after work and thought, Sweet Jesus, is this place a mess. I hate coming home. The entrance is through my kitchen. There were shreds and chips of wood, empty cans of ravioli, old jelly jars striated with wine residue, a roach's corpse. I could remember when the white enamel of the old appliances would catch my eye. In the living room, the hide-a-bed oozed quilts and pillows, socks and jockey shorts. There were shoeboxes full of figures I'd carved but hadn't gotten around to painting, brushes and knives, forks and corkscrews. I'd have to lift the trouser's leg if I wanted to watch TV. Kitchen, living room, and bath for a hundred and a half a month. It'll do. But I can't keep the place up.

At least I know where the sugar and the chili powder are. I can find the extra toilet paper and the Raid. Back issues of *Arizona Highways* and *Colorado* and *Alaska Outdoors* are in the credenza my landlord bought a year ago. The travel guides guests at Pilgrim's Harbor leave behind are stacked on the pantry floor with the Rand McNally's and the Sunset books of beautiful places. Once in a while, I pull together the sheets and towels, sack up the dirty clothes, and spend a morning at the laundromat. It just doesn't hold my attention. Back when I was seeing Nikki, we had it tidied up. But I haven't put much into it since then.

Not that I think the apartment itself is bad. Upstairs living, for instance, has a lot to recommend it. No footsteps on the ceiling, no sway in the light fixtures or leaks from overflowing bathtubs above me. I hardly ever see the old woman from downstairs, Mrs. Heaney, except for once a day when she stands in her doorway to watch me leave for Pilgrim's Harbor.

When I turned back from the window to the clutter, it made me realize how artificial the notion of home really is. People ask me if I'm going home after work. That makes me laugh. This? I don't leave work to go home.

What I do in the apartment is *functuate*, putting in my time doing the tasks, filling in the space. I interimize.

Some people functuate behind laminated particle-board desks in fluorescent lit offices hoping someday to get a window and a blackboard. Some people functuate in front of a classroom discussing the influence of the Franco-Prussian War on nineteenth century European literature and economics, as glassy-eyed as their students. I functuate here, at home, doing my poor imitation of man at leisure.

What I do at Pilgrim's Harbor is, quite literally, my living.

The apartment's other window is in the bathroom above the stool. A person would have to stand on the tank to see where I park my Pinto under the carport in back. It wouldn't be worth it.

I only need the carport space when the other people are gone. If I'm not in the apartment or at work, I'm usually at the Westview Center Shopping Mall. It's about a mile past the interstate, visible from the overpass.

Westview is huge. It's shaped like a starfish with the big department stores at the ends of each arm and an assortment of restaurants, snack bars, and a tavern circling the central disk. The rest is standard mall, everything anybody in the region needed except a mortician, car wash, and church.

If I try, I can accomplish the Westview Day: everything I wear, eat, drink, read, and talk to in one day could come from Westview. Stationed outside the Spur n' Saddle with a glass of Oly Gold, I can watch the people below as they stand under the plastic trees, or nibble cheese popcorn while they walk on the mock-brick floors. It's not the dull diversion that it might sound like. I'm off tomorrow and plan to blow my afternoon there.

***

I had this friend in Lancaster, Pennsylvania, when I was about eight. He had the goofy name—Eben Mannlich—and I had the distinction of being the newcomer in school, so we gravitated to each other.

Eben lived in a house on Race Avenue that has always stood for Home in my fantasies. This was the house of houses, to my way of thinking. Remembering the Mannlich's home still warms me like a bowl of farina on a winter morning.

Eben and I would run up the walk to the front door, careful not to step on the lawn. That was one thing right there—respect for the grounds. We'd always push open the huge oak door together, so I was never really certain one person alone could do it. Inside, along with the rush of warmth, was a foyer.

Mrs. Mannlich pronounced it Foi-ay, with a wisp of smoke escaping from her exquisitely rounded lips. Dr. Mannlich, who taught German at the college, pronounced it fancier still, Fwa-yay, like a true Frenchman. It was a lovely space in which to collect ourselves, to quiet down and be suitably mature for the rest of the house.

I remember the old light fixtures and a hat rack on the wall in the foyer, where there was always a red plaid scarf hung to be grabbed if the day was unexpectedly cold, an umbrella waiting against the occasion of rain.

There was also a rug in the foyer, the kind we would never have had in my own house, or if we did we couldn't walk on it. The Mannliches used it to wipe the soles of their shoes on before entering the house proper.

Although there were several choices to make when leaving the foyer—down to the living room, up to the bedrooms, straight ahead to the eating area—I only have clear recall of heading up. Most of our time together was spent in Eben's bedroom, lying on the floor, playing penny baseball. The house always smelled of spices. It always tasted of chocolate. There was always music.

CHAPTER EIGHT

I once heard somebody say there are two classes of travel in America—first class and with children. I've seen enough to support that theory.

A couple came in with two kids, traveling back home from a trip to British Columbia. It was the kind of trip in which they didn't mind going a few hundred miles out of their way just to see something special, the meteor crater in northern Arizona or the Taos Pueblo. They went down to Santa Rosa to visit her parents, came back up through Reno to rendezvous with his brother, and swooped past the Great Salt Lake. It was a long summer tour.

The Meyers were a nice couple, early thirties, kids

well behaved. I didn't worry about where to put them, like I do over some families that traveled with eight and ten year olds.

Mr. Meyer was always touching one of the kids and Mrs. Meyer was very calm. They managed to refuse giving the kids change for the candy machine without making them whine or yell. That was real control. Jerry and Nancy.

I gave them two keys, one for each child, and spoke with the parents, who seemed glad for adult company. They had spent a night on the way to Santa Rosa in Garberville, at a motel called Sherwood Forest. I figured the name had something to do with Garberville being near the redwoods.

They said the motel was set up on a hill with some rooms near the top and a driveway that curved down around a heated pool to more rooms near the bottom. Spacious place.

As they spoke, it was as if the Meyers were seeing again the strange child riding his bicycle breakneck down the hill and around a curve, screeching to a stop just before a row of parked cars in front of the rooms below. He had a hoarse voice and no color except in his windblown cheeks, wore thick glasses and a plaid shirt buttoned at the collar. He marched back up the hill, careened with his hair straight up in the wind, letting go a long whoop as he sped down with wide-opened eyes.

The Meyers had been clucking and talking about how dangerous that boy's behavior was while the family changed for dinner. I could picture the four of them knotting their ties and bows, shaking their heads, learning their lessons behind the closed door in Sherwood Forest.

When they walked out to the Eel River Cafe, they heard a horrible scream, more a cluster of shrieks, and Jerry said he ran down the hill toward the noise. The strange kid was lying tangled in his bike, bleeding badly from his nose, mouth, and ears, sustaining his awful wail that finally brought his parents and grandparents from their room.

Jerry said the kid was hurt so badly he was sure he'd never recover. It took the ambulance twenty minutes to get there. They could hear it coming while they waited for dinner.

They gave the kids the seminar on safety and got them to promise never to ride fast downhill. It was clear to me that the Meyers spent the whole night in tears.

I watched the four of them unload the car in front of #44, full of joy at working together, and felt oddly sad. I don't often let myself be saddened by my guests' stories, though many of them are riddled with misery.

Lives pass through Pilgrim's Harbor, people come in and out of my life, and sometimes it seems that all there is is more of the same. The Meyers were hobbled by seeing that kid in Garberville. They appeared to limp as they headed over to Harbor Side. I'd wager they'll drive straight home from now on, no side trips through the Badlands or Rushmore.

If it had been my motel, no kid would be riding his bike like a maniac down the hill. I look after the guests.

***

This won't be a bad weekend. Most people will be on the road next weekend and resting up on this one.

The week before a holiday like the Fourth, Pilgrim's

Harbor gets only the serious traveler. They're more appreciative of quality hospitality, less fooled by the glitter and the deals. It will be a welcomed prelude to the next week. Complaints skyrocket on the holidays, with the guests really wanting home instead of refuge.

A guest came in who was a member of the American Cavern Keepers Association, a traveler in earnest. I've seen people from an astounding number of associations. In the last year alone, I've met card-carrying members of Turtles International Association, Sweet Adelines, the Baker Street Irregulars, Izaak Walton League, GASP, and Deltiologists of America. Everyone's in some club. They just won't always tell you about it.

When I get a guest wearing the ring or the hat, or with the insignia on the jacket, I know he's going to talk about the organization even before he checks to see if the room is all right. But I understand. I've just joined the National Wood Carvers Association and read their *Chip Chats* cover to cover.

This guest was from Corydon, Indiana. Big chapter there. He was involved with the Marengo Cave, Wyandotte, Squire Boone Caverns, even as far north as Blue Springs Caverns.

The ACKA figures out model lighting arrangements, does scripts for guides, comes up with names for the different formations and features in a cavern—Devil's Eyelet, Crystal Waterfall, Garden of Ice. They deal with insurance issues, utilities, earth retention. They make good signs, supply trinkets, offer a half dozen options to enhance the basic cavern tour.

Clarence "Rock" Robertson gave me a pack of brochures for my display and said it didn't matter if they were 1,200 miles or so from his territory. There was a list of member caverns in the back.

Rock spoke harshly about what he called The Merchants, people who combined their cavern tours with little amusement parks or tourist traps like petting zoos and graveyards. John Wilkes Booth and Jesse James couldn't possibly have hidden out in half the caves that claimed them. The Merchants were undermining the pure cavern keeping industry.

I mentioned that the Pruitts once considered putting a little amusement park behind Pilgrim's Harbor. They thought about buying into a few rides, some pop the balloon or knock over the bottle games, elephant ear stands. They explored tying up a baby goat or llama for the kids to feed, maybe a sow with piglets.

I was against it, but didn't say anything to the Pruitts. Why run the risk of making the guests angry? Nobody likes to look bad with a baseball in front of the family. But the Pruitts didn't believe Dewey Howser was hired to be a thinker.

I would have moved on if they'd done it. Imagine the guests with their prize pink elephants, their backscratchers and tambourines, stepping in llama dung and goat pellets. Lots of maintenance problems there. Mercifully, the idea did itself in without my having to fight it.

That was why I was so comfortable with Rock Robertson. We had the same views on gimmicks.

Robertson said there was a strong chapter in Pennsylvania, several out west, and was heading for the annual conference in Missouri next month. Those are places I like. Maybe I should join up.

I imagined that I could see, when Robertson yawned, stalactites and stalagmites in the man's throat. That he was cold and clammy to shake hands with. Dark eyes. He made a noise every few minutes, clearing his nose like he had a constant sinus drip. His head looked like it had been smoothed by too many people touching it. Maybe that's why he's so short.

***

Pilgrim's Harbor didn't fill up tonight. I kept hoping Finfer would get in touch, though I knew he wouldn't have reached Woonsocket yet. But maybe he called ahead, heard about the briefcase, and been put out of his worry. I was anxious to get the thing on its way, to reach closure on the matter.

By the time I left for my apartment, I was feeling sort of melancholy. Lonely, as if friends I'd expected hadn't showed and never called. This happened to me from time to time, an occupational hazard.

I felt like I hadn't had my share of conversation, like the game I had tickets for was rained out, like my blind date wouldn't come downstairs, like the steelhead weren't biting.

And I'm off tomorrow. Maybe that's it.

Couldn't go anywhere far, have been everywhere near, nothing special planned. Maybe I'll carve something big, a statue for out front of the office or right inside the door where guests can enjoy it when they register. Maybe two, a set. Pioneer family, or a cowboy with six-guns and a pilgrim lady six feet tall. Something American.

CHAPTER NINE

I had coffee and two bear claws at Winchell's in Westview Center. Arriving too late to watch the fountains come on, I had to make do with *The Courier*.

The metal screens and glass doors rolled open at the storefronts. A workman from TRANCO got the escalator started and climbed out of the trap at its bottom. A group of teenagers set up chairs and a stage in the middle of the lower level. I began to lose track of the time.

A few couples with young children were on the same schedule I was. They strolled, nibbling donuts, waiting for 9:30. Wes Handy began knocking out tunes on his new organ, a big Lowery with hundreds of knobs. All day, in every corner of the mall, people would be hearing Wes' tunes. From "Take Me Out To the Ballgame" to "Moon River," they suggested a roller rink more than a retail oasis.

A mall at this time of day is like a highway motel around 3:00. Getting its rhythm going, starting all its elements toward accommodation, opening up. This is one of my favorite times at Westview Center, although 3:00 at Pilgrim's Harbor makes me restless as a small child in a car.

At the mall, the preparatory sounds and sights please me. I'll nod at the owners and kids who run the stores, since I know most of them but there's no need to make them comfortable, to see if they require cheer. After a day off, what always feels most rested is my voice.

I ate a hot pretzel with mustard and cheese spread, and headed for my spot by the Spur n' Saddle to wash it down with a Coke. I'd hold off on the Oly Gold till noon.

***

When I saw the young woman, my first reaction was to look away quickly. She was half turned from me, but I didn't trust myself to look at her again.

Instead, I looked at myself. As if disembodied and hanging over the railing above, I watched myself reel. It was like being at the dentist's office, getting a shot of novocaine in my mouth—the sensation of excruciating warmth, liquid heat introduced into a place so private that the violation is extraordinary—and then going numb. That numbness made such fine sense. This was what I felt through the middle of my chest now, as if shot deep with novocaine, soon to grow numb.

Then I thought, Be careful. Remember the child who gnaws through his novocained lip after having his tooth extracted. What couldn't be felt accurately at first can come back shortly as agony.

But the body heals. I looked back at her.

She looked 19, but it was possible that she was 36. What got me was the poise, the utter self-containment in the way she stood looking at the Mall Directory.

She seemed interested rather than anxious. She was also quite at ease not knowing where to find what she wanted. Some people hunch over the directory, using a finger to find their destination, tension evident in every gesture. But she seemed to relax, to settle a bit onto her heels. I leaned forward to watch where she would go.

I could see how precisely her blonde hair was parted, its exact taper back to the nape, its rich health. She had the wide, rounded shoulders of a distance swimmer. Although I appreciate women's bodies, their form, I hadn't understood the notion of figure before.

This woman had a figure, all right, astounding in its balance and emphasis. In tight white jeans, her hips reminded me of those I would see in my beginner's guide to carving, almost too symmetrical in their roundness. The dark belt called attention to a waist I thought I could ring with my thumb and forefinger.

Her simple shirt was pale blue, the color of summer sky. She had on ankle-high socks and a pair of old, pink running shoes.

She turned so quickly, and looked directly up at me as if my attention had been palpable to her, that I was without defense. No smile, no looking away, just me gaping and gawking like the lecher I'd been transformed into. She held my stare.

"Were you making silly sounds too?"

"No, those I could control."

"I want to look at the dogs." She pointed over her shoulder at the directory.

"This level," I said. "Over by Sears."

We didn't attract any attention. Although she spoke in a voice slightly above disco-party level and I tried not to shout over the thirty feet between us, no one seemed to hear us. I gulped the Coke, met her at the top of the stairs, and fell into step beside her.

"Pet stores in malls," she said.

"It's mostly fish."

"Still."

"I thought it was pretty common."

"That doesn't make it acceptable, you know. Tuberculosis was pretty common too."

"In malls?"

She missed, at most, two beats. I felt that I was holding my own.

"The plan is," she said, "I'm going to buy a dog a month as long as I'm around here. Clean them up, worm them, housebreak them, then give them to kids at the junior college."

"How long are you planning to be here for? I mean, are we talking about a multi-year program, with the advertisements and the word-of-mouth?"

"Who knows?"

"I wonder if there'll be takers."

"What kind of kid wouldn't take a dog?"

"I mean the cost. JC kids might not be able to afford

the food and shots."
"No way." She waved my foolishness right out through the skylight.
"OK, I'll buy one also."
"Why's that?"
"For the cause."
She slackened her pace and turned to look at me. There was almost a smile, a hint of new color in her cheeks and at her neck.
"Dogs in malls," she said.
"I know. I'm against it."
"What else are you against?"
"Oh, lots of things, I'm a very activist person. Tuberculosis, discount air fares, unrequited love."
"Slow down," she said, not without warmth.
"Right. How about I help you pick out a dog?"
She began to walk again, but slower. I noticed the small pearl flush against her earlobe. I wouldn't have minded helping to fasten it in place. With my teeth.
"You don't look to me like a dog person."
"What kind of person do I look like?"
"An indoor person. Parakeet in a cage, or maybe a gerbil in an old aquarium."
"That's close. I operate a motel."
"That's a new angle."
"We don't allow dogs in the rooms. I apologize."
I'd finally made her smile. At least her teeth weren't straight and fulsome. I might be able to keep talking to her.
"I wouldn't either. In your business."
"Listen, before we go in: I'm Dewey."
She stopped again. Her amusement seemed wildly erotic. But we were in front of Pet World and she began to be distracted.
"And I'm Snowflake."

"No, I mean it. Duane Howser. So, Dewey."

"Cindy Bonds. Oh, look at that. Half those black mollies will be belly up by the time McDonald's stops serving Egg McMuffins."

I looked where she was pointing. When I looked back, she had spun in the opposite direction. She was studying the birds on display.

"Black mollies?" I said. "I thought they were guppies."

"And look at these. Nobody out here buys budgies. They'll have 20 more next month. What do they do with them?"

By the time I turned again to look at the crowd of birds, Cindy was gone, headed full-stride for the puppies. She was certainly good at keeping me off balance.

I still hadn't had time to savor her shape close up, to stand back enough from the movement and the torrent of speech in order to admire her fullness and grace. I ran a hand through my hair, then patted it in place although it never got messy.

I followed back to the dogs. She was bent at the waist, almost ninety degrees, face to face with a Terrier pup.

The pup broke away from her gaze to chase his tail. I struggled not to put my hands on Cindy's hips, to push up against her haunches, and be as bold as she was making me feel. Instead, I bent over and made kissing sounds at the pup.

"Dewey," Cindy said.

"At your service."

"No, him. He should be called Dewey, not you. Look at him."

"Why?"

"His eyes."

"I'd call him Beady, not Dewey."
"I'd think a motel operator would have a quicker eye for character."
I didn't respond, trying to assess if this had been a wrong turn.
"Moving right along, I think his coat could use some help, don't you?"
"He just needs exercise." The pup began to wiggle with delight, thinking she was talking to him.
"And a brushing."
"Just some hands in his fur." She puckered her lips and squeaked out a kiss.
"If he's Dewey, who should I be?"
"Don't know yet. Before, I would have said Ernest. But there may be some hope yet. You could turn out to be a Clint or a Claude, anything's possible."
"Are you taking the dog with you?"
Since it was Dewey, I was rooting for the Terrier. I could certainly see the benefit in being cleaned, groomed, and housebroken by someone as concerned with my happiness as Cindy Bonds.
"The Saint is nice, you don't often see them in pet stores. But they're impossible to unload. This Beagle's a little lopsided; kids would love him. And the mixed is cute but there's something wrong with her foot. I don't know."
She stood erect, done with her quick analysis. She slipped her hands into her back pockets.
I could hear the hands move down in there, against her butt. Maybe it was not having a countertop between us, or not having the familiar business of registration and keys to rely on, but I was feeling unsteady now that our conversation had lasted over a half-hour.
"I can tell the Terrier likes you."

Maybe I shouldn't have offered advice. But I didn't have the patience to let things take their time and go their natural course because I'd already decided where I wanted them to end up.

Then she said, "Easy, Dewey. You may get to come with me too, I hear you, but let me get the right dog."

So she knew. All I have to do is be a good lad.

"Not a word," I promised.

"One thing at a time."

I turned away. Four hamsters were asleep all over each other, surrounded by lettuce. Birds cheeped. Aquariums bubbled.

I was ready to jump and try clicking my heels. But I didn't think I should distract Cindy just then.

***

She consented to eat with me. Pet World would hold the Beagle until Cindy was ready to pick him up.

Buying lunch for a vegetarian was a challenge in Westview Center. We headed for the central disk.

"Nothing fried, either," she said.

"Salad Bar? There's one in Lindstrom's."

"Let's have a look at it."

We had to half-circle the central disk. Chip, the waiter at Spur n' Saddle, winked at me when we passed.

"Do you eat eggs?"

"Sure. I'm an ovolacto."

"Funny, I'd have guessed you were Dutch."

"Milk, eggs." She seemed engrossed in thought and was staring at the shops with a frown. "I just don't eat meat."

"Even if it flies?"

"Or swims."

Lindstrom's is all mirrors and clear plastic. Mirrors up the walls, plastic tables and chairs you can see through, and a clear plastic pushcart for the salad bar. It's difficult to get dimensions right in the place. Everything floats.

Cindy walked to the salad bar, scanning the items, their bowls nestled in ice. She slipped her hands into the back pockets again, her posture for contemplation, and shook her head sadly.

"Look at this garbage."

Like when she first called to me from the Mall Directory, Cindy seemed able to converse over distances without attracting listeners, as if her voice were on a different frequency than the one to which most people were tuned. None of the patrons digging at their plates of salad turned to stare.

I stood next to her, blushing, but determined to keep up with her.

Nothing in the salad bar held its true color. Brown had equal time with green all through the lettuce bowl, at best the tomatoes could be called pink, the radishes were flecked with black, and the impression made by the bean sprouts was that they were mushrooms. The only thing looking like it should was the chunked ham laced with fat.

"Look at this," she said. "Nothing but iceberg lettuce. None of these places ever has leaves."

"I never noticed that."

"And canned mushrooms. God, you can go out and pick enough morels around here to stock a dozen salad bars, and they give you Del Monte."

"What's with the celery tidbits?"

I thought it would be good to join in the attack. We'd circled the salad bar and were back by the stack of frozen plates.

"The food processor at work. At least they left the skin on the carrots. Give credit where credit is due."

"Let's find another place."

"I can't eat salad with plastic forks. The noise is too creepy."

Some patrons had stopped eating by the time I began to add my observations. They watched and through the transparent tables it looked as if they were levitating.

"Drinks in paper cups," I said, with as much contempt as I could muster.

Cindy bumped my arm as we left. She smelled faintly of clove. Every hair on my other arm tingled, I swear it was possible to feel each one.

"Any more suggestions, Ace?" she asked.

"All's not lost. Let's check the soup of the day at the Spur n' Saddle. The vegetable's good and so was the lentil the only time I tried it."

"Home made?"

"Sign says so."

Cindy told me she'd begun working at the county hospital, nights. She was new to the area and was going to enroll at the college part-time next quarter, learn something else to do. I wasn't certain I understood what she did at the hospital, though it seemed to have something to do with computers. I also wasn't clear on what she wanted to study at the college.

For a person who seemed to be telling you something, she sure didn't give much in the way of facts. She'd make a great guest at the motel.

"You have to be careful with the soup in these places," she said. "They usually use beef stock, or put sausage in the lentil soup. Most people won't eat it if it's straight vegetarian."

The soup at Spur n' Saddle was chicken noodle. Chip winked at me again and was obviously rooting for my success with the new blonde. He'd given my usual seat to somebody else.

"We could get a foot-long," I suggested. "I'd eat the hot dog and you could stuff the bun with condiments."

"Yum."

"They've got great relish, nice chunks of onion, cole slaw, kraut. A feast."

"Those buns never have grain in them. I don't know how people can eat them."

"There's always pizza."

"You're not rising to the challenge."

For all I knew, we could have been walking in circles. I was in a daze.

We stopped in front of Heart & Sole, the runners' store, and I touched her arm lightly enough to make her stop but not so hard as to seem pushy. She turned toward me.

"What did you plan to do for lunch before I came along?" I asked.

"To skip it. My morning granola's usually enough to hold me."

She waved to someone behind me, inside the store. The guy who sells the Adidas, tall and lean with hair to his shoulders and beard to his chest, dressed in blue sweats, waved a shoe at her.

I glared at him. Probably runs fifteen miles each way, to and from work.

"We could buy some cheese at The Barnyard. Package of Wheat Thins." I began to worry that, as I had with Crissy Chrysler at Pilgrim's Harbor, I was losing Cindy through a lack of proficiency at repartee.

"Processed junk. Tell you what, let's pick up stuff at the health store. Malls always have one, there should be something edible besides pills."

"Like?"

"Yogurt. Nuts and raisins, some dried fruits."

"Sounds enchanting. Papaya juice to drink."

She elbowed me. I realized we were the same height. She had seemed larger.

"Apple's fine."

"What do I know?"

I was glad to leave the Heart & Sole window. To Your Health was located near where I first saw her and we went down without speaking. She stopped by a drinking fountain.

"Do you have a sweet tooth?" she asked.

"Not really. My tastes run toward plate lunches and take out dinners."

"Pity. You could use the bulk."

I didn't remember her looking me over closely enough to tell. I flexed my biceps.

"I keep a set of dumbbells in the office."

She chuckled and looked toward the skylights. I checked to be sure there were no crumbs on my clothes from breakfast.

I still hadn't told her anything about Pilgrim's Harbor. She judged quickly and I thought she might disapprove.

I took her hand.

"You ever bake bread?" she asked.

"From scratch?"

"That's what you need to do, of course. It'll strengthen your hands. Something sticky, like oatmeal bread; be just the thing."

We tried samples of jasmine tea and trail mix at the entrance to To Your Health. I took a wire handbasket and Cindy dropped her selections in. She popped two Vitamin C tablets into my mouth while the cashier worked on lunch.

"Too bad you don't have a sweet tooth. I'd split one of those coconut macaroons with you."

"I'll force myself. For the bulk."

I paid. Cindy took the sack and we headed back the way we'd come.

"Let's eat outside," she said.

"In the parking lot?"

"Drive me to some woods."

I couldn't have said it any better myself. We strolled out to the car and were struck by the thick June heat. It reminded me that I prefer to spend my off days inside the mall.

Cindy's energy was enough to carry us. I would just hang on. I didn't have to be anywhere until tomorrow.

***

"Tell me about this motel of yours."

We sat in a field of long grass by the reservoir. The grass was parched and flowed in the warm breeze.

Balanced on thick tires and stacks of bricks, an abandoned logging wagon without sides served as seat and table. We were side by side, passing the yogurt back and forth. The Beagle pup slept beside her, on an old towel from the trunk of my car.

The drive had been quiet, as if Cindy required time to decompress after her two hours in Westview Center. She was changed by the outdoors, noticeably more relaxed and quiet.

Choosing between the risks of boring her or intruding, I kept silent and let her study the landscape. I remembered, and heeded, the advice once given by a Pilgrim's Harbor guest from Vermont: you shouldn't talk unless you can improve the silence.

As soon as it came into view, the reservoir had just the effect I had hoped in choosing it as the destination. Cindy opened like a shamrock.

"Right," she had said.

"Sullivan Reservoir. It's either here or drive up to the clear-cut. Let's eat."

I had never eaten with a woman of such lusty appetite. She liked chewing two dried fruits at once—fig and apricot, or date and prune—and took nuts a fistful at a time. It wasn't impolite or gross. She ate slowly, steadily, and watching her made me hungrier.

"I didn't like the valley."

I was already used to her way of starting conversations out-of-the-blue, a few sentences deep into whatever she had been thinking about. It was invigorating to try and keep up with her.

"It's supposed to be postcard pretty," I said. She shook her head. "What, too much rain?"

"Nah, that's a myth about the valley. Rains lightly but a lot." She licked yogurt off her spoon like ice cream. "No real bother."

"What else have I heard . . . it's an area wholly owned by the special interests, some guest told me." My knowledge base was coming in handy. "The wine people, the real estate people, venture capitalists."

"I don't know. It was a long time ago, before I was aware of what went on. Anyhow, all the good kids went north. There wasn't much to stay around for."

"And you came here."

"Eventually. For a job and some new space."

She kicked her legs idly. Her breasts, on their own under the pale shirt, moved in time with her legs. With her tongue poked in between her upper teeth and lip, she dangled her head back to watch the clouds.

She knew I was watching. She considered and decided it was all right.

"Well, we do have space."

Cindy unwrapped the macaroon and laid it on her lap. She pressed her thumb into its top, murmuring "good, it's soft." As her thumb penetrated, the macaroon split neatly in half.

"I can also juggle," she said. "And read tea leaves."

"Where were you before the valley?"

"Portland. Yakima two years. Billings and Coeur d'Alene. Like that."

So she was not 19. I waited to see how much she was ready to reveal.

"I am a person," she said with a chuckle, "who actually grew up in Walla Walla."

"The town they liked so much they named it twice?"

"Father was the warden at the prison."

"Was?"

"Now he farms. Wheat and green peas." She chuckled again. "And he crowds a lot of pigs into a few pens."

Then suddenly, as she did almost everything, she thrust the conversation away from herself. She asked about the motel. I drew back slightly. She stopped kicking and lay down on the boards of the old wagon as if ready for a bed time story.

It was a gesture of invitation that had little of the sexual in it. Take it away, Dewey Howser.

"We drove past it on the way. Pilgrim's Harbor, right

by the interstate."

"Why didn't you point it out?"

"I don't know. You seemed preoccupied."

"If you're going to get to know me, you're going to have to adapt to that. I'm always preoccupied." She reached over and patted my leg. "Pre-occupied."

"Fair enough."

"Now, do you own this Pilgrim's Haven?"

"Harbor. No. I just run it. But I could see owning a place some day."

I hadn't planned to say that yet. It must be the fresh air. We were not in the kind of field that a person wanted to walk through. It was a sitting field. Cows lowed in the distance, mountains were visible, but not overly assertive, in a semi-circle to the south. I felt ready to stay for days, which was not a familiar feeling.

"What would it be like, your own place?"

"Oh, small. Keep turning guests over. No one could stay more than one night, no one could eat more than two meals there, that sort of thing. Transiency elevated to the ideal. And I'd do away with end rooms."

"You know, I can't tell when you're teasing and when you're honest. I don't remember liking that feeling before."

"I'm doing both, Cindy."

"Have you ever had somebody famous stay at the motel?"

"Most famous people use their fame to avoid driving anywhere near here. But Mickey Mantle stayed once, about two years back. Even ate at Harbor Side."

"Mickey Mantle? Doesn't he do TV commercials?"

"When I was a kid, Mantle was a great baseball player. The story is, he abused his body. Anyway, I asked him why he was staying at Pilgrim's Harbor instead of the Holiday Inn 30 miles up. He looked at me like I was a dumb sportswriter in the clubhouse and all he said was 'Ah'm tahrd.'"

"Sounds like quite the wit."

"You had to be there."

We bagged the trash, stuffed it against one tire so it wouldn't blow away, and walked to the edge of the reservoir. The ridge of mountains, without a trace of snow, seemed closer than usual.

It was past 3:00. I had no idea what to suggest. I don't know how long we stood there looking separate ways.

"I like you," she said, out of nowhere. "Let me see your motel."

"When?" It was half question, half blurt.

"Now, on the way back into town."

"I was thinking . . . "

"I know what you were thinking. But no more today."

"It's still early, though."

"Dewey, I don't have a phone yet, I have to paint the rooms, I have to set up the kitchen." She turned to me and smiled. "Ah'm tahrd."

"I could help. Paint, I mean, and like that."

"You'll get a chance. I'll reach you when I become reachable." She pointed back toward the car. "I will."

"We haven't decided what to name the dog."

"We won't. I will. In a few days, after I've lived with him a while."

"Suppose we get lost on the way back?" I said.

"Car could find Pilgrim's Harbor without you."

***

That evening, I couldn't stay around my apartment. I made a half-hearted attempt at cleaning up, starting with the kitchen. But it was going to take more effort than I was able to give. Just doing the cans and jelly jars wore me out. The surfaces would have to wait.

I glanced distractedly through the new issue of *The Ohio Motorist* that I'd found a few days ago. Neither "Power Packing: The Fine Art of Getting More in Your Trunk" nor "Pickaway County Days" held my interest, so I tossed the magazine away.

What I really should do is buy a stereo system, something small, maybe just a portable tape recorder and a few jazz cassettes. Some day, there'll be the right sale at Westview and I will.

For an hour, I carved. It was pleasant to feel the fit of a small chunk of pine in my hand, though the tools still hurt my fingertips because I never worked at carving long enough to get callused. The face I'd been puttering with for months wasn't going anywhere.

I tried to move through the maze of my thoughts in a systematic way. I recognized that Cindy had happened by chance. In my experience, chance encounters were best kept to under 12 hours. That prospect didn't excite me.

Next, I remembered that I had to be cautious. I'd only recently started to feel that everything was under control again. So it wouldn't do to lose control over Cindy.

But I supposed it would be all right to feel a little excited by a beautiful blonde woman who was a) willing to spend all day with me, and b) promising to call me when she was reachable.

Nothing I can do but wait. She made me drop her

off at the mall and promise not to follow. She said she'd get home, she said she'd get in touch.
I know it'll be days. Meanwhile, business as usual at Pilgrim's Harbor. Mustn't functuate. Besides, with the Fourth coming up, there's plenty of work to be done.

***

At nine, I went back to Westview Center and saw a movie because I wanted popcorn and cool air. They recently remodeled Cinema Two into Cinema Four, but haven't changed the sign yet. As soon as they do, it'll probably be remodeled into Cinema Six.

Fancy seats were added to all four theaters. They're like the seats in French movie houses and I enjoy leaning back, resting the head, getting lost. Can't remember what picture I saw, though, which isn't a good sign. Maybe I slept through it.

A little Hearty Burgundy back at the apartment and I was thinking about Cindy again. Her image was clear as it had been in the instant before she turned to catch me staring.

Ordinarily, I might hold that image. I might use it to launch a drowsy fantasy as I moved toward sleep. But I shied away this time, thinking you can jinx a fantasy if you're not careful.

***

The dream was wonderful.

I was living in a mountain town. It was summer, but the night was cool. There was a woman named Ruth—I knew because there was a nameplate beside her door, as in a school. She was tall and slender, a muscular, beautiful woman.

She had once been a world-class platform diver, an Olympic hopeful, graceful and breathtaking. Then she was in a motorcycle accident and injured her legs so badly that she was confined to a wheelchair for the rest of her life. Everybody, apparently, knew Ruth's story.

But in this dream, I was able to get her out of the wheelchair because of her love for me. I don't know what I said, but she just rose up and smiled, reaching her hands out for me. It seems to me now there was rousing music.

She limped with me to the top of a cliff above the river where it was cold enough that snow dusted the trail and made the ledge treacherous. But she trusted me and somewhere along the way she became nude.

I took photographs of her diving. She arched and twisted, plunging toward the water, entering without splash. I developed the photos, blew them up, studied with her the classic beauty of her form.

I knew she loved to hear me discuss her body in action. In an instant, I had printed captions below her favorites, with an emphasis on the erotic. Ruth then lay on the bed and adopted the same postures that had been caught by my camera.

Lying on her side, her left leg kicking toward her head, she imitated the moment in which her dive began. Her arms were flexed as in the instant before being outspread. I could see her from every angle at once.

She lay like that and I entered her from behind.

CHAPTER TEN

Now that I've worked at Pilgrim's Harbor over five years, I get four meals a year free at Harbor Side. I'm also entitled to a dinner at Christmas, but not *on* Christmas; a dinner closer to Passover than Easter; and either breakfast or brunch two other times of my choice.

This plan led me to conclude that lunch had to be the best meal. I decided today to test out this theory.

If the lunch was even half as good as the four other meals I had from them this year, it'd be far better than my usual pack of peanuts and microwaved burrito. It was worth a shot.

From my apartment, I called Ellie Suggs, who runs Harbor Side, at 11:00 to be sure I got my order in soon enough. It was hard to make sensible choices since I didn't have a menu in front of me. I need those pictures to make sense out of items like Gobbler's Delight (How could I ask Ellie if that's turkey, or something that turkeys like to eat?), Peasant Under Grass, or Poor Man's Scampi.

At 2:00, I walked to Harbor Side to pick up the food. Ellie had my Peasant Under Grass (chicken sandwich with slaw) in one bag, my pickle in a second, container of potato salad in a third, can of Coke in a fourth, and peanut butter cookie in a fifth. Then all five bags were inside a sixth.

"Good thing this is only lunch for one," I said.

"Policy is policy."

"Ever heard of Saran Wrap?"

"Don't be fresh, Dewey. At least we don't put little strips of paper over the toilet seat."

"Tell me why I don't get any free lunches with my five-year food package."

"You'll have to ask Jock Pruitt. I think it's because he always eats lunch here and doesn't want to risk eating with you."

I left and resisted tearing into lunch until I'd gotten back to my office. Going over the week's paperwork, waiting for the last rooms to be cleaned so the maids could leave, I was able to drag lunch out to 3:30. What I should have done was throw it away at 2:10.

Ellie was wrong. The reason they don't give us free lunches is because the food is bad enough to kill the help.

I figure Pruitt's theory has to be that lunch is for the locals. Guests arrive in time for dinner and usually include breakfast before hitting the road. This is one tightly budgeted investment.

***

About 7:30, a green Ford wagon pulled in. It was packed so full of camping gear, the rear window bulged when the car came up the driveway.

Pilgrim's Harbor occasionally gets big families, mostly in August before the kids go back to school. They arrive after camping for two straight weeks and are only looking for a bed, a shower, TV, a door with a knob. Civilization.

Whenever I see them, I think about how the bathrooms will look in the morning. High on the staff gripe list is the overloaded room, the family package.

Campers prove I don't need to get out there and rough it. Thanks to them, I now know all I need to about bouncing through National Forest campgrounds in a loaded station wagon looking for the last unoccupied parking spot. I know about being a tent camper in a KOA with motorcyclists beside you in some Adair, Iowa, city park on top of a railroad overpass. Enough people come to Pilgrim's Harbor after a sleepless night on the banks of a river they had planned to canoe, complaining about the all-night party four trees down that kept them awake.

I don't see happy campers. I see miserable campers forced to spend the night in a motel they won't admit they stayed in once they get home.

The worst camping case so far was an elderly couple two summers ago, a pair of RV'ers. They're probably the guests most responsible for my irrational feelings about campers.

Ethel and Enos Pletch out of Elkhorn City, Kentucky, by the Breaks of the Sandy. They were pulling a 25-foot Airstream. Old Enos popped out of the driver's side of the big blue Mercury like a cork from a bottle and landed in the office so fast I thought he was going to charge right through the counter.

He was two levels above rage, where a person starts to get quiet and compact with his fury. But he also gets so red you're sure he's going to be stained forever.

Ethel strolled in behind him, talking sweetly about home while Enos struggled to find breath. She was thin and long-armed, with elbows that were the size of most people's knees. She wore a warm smile.

"It'll be nice to get home, papa. We didn't see anything on the whole trip that could compare to home. Won't it be nice to get home, papa?"

Her voice was smooth and her words seemed like a quilt she'd worked on for years to wrap around her husband in his worst times. She had a lovely head of gray hair in a bun and the thin hands of a china painter.

"I'm not spending another night in that tin can," he whispered. "Tuna's all that belongs in one of those things."

"It was nice of the Mortons to lend it to us."

"Jimmy Tim Morton probably planned this for ten

years. Figured I'd die off on a trip like this and then he'd buy our house for cheap."

"Enos has a bad heart," Ethel explained. "This vacation was to be therapeutic. But I guess it's time to head home, now."

I didn't classify them as hardened campers. So I gave them #17. I thought Pletch could park around the side and not have to see the Airstream from his window.

But it didn't help. Pletch was back an hour after checking in, his face the color of good Kentucky clay.

"Are you all right?"

I don't keep much besides aspirin around, but they sell a few things up at Harbor Side. Pletch looked like he'd need something compounded by a person with a certificate on the wall.

"Back home there's this gorge, the Grand Canyon of the South. It's where Russell Fork goes over into the Big Sandy, a fifteen hundred foot shot. You know the kind of hole I mean?"

I nodded.

"Well, I've been dreaming for three weeks about that Airstream going over. It's driving me nuts."

He left without saying another word. Half hour later he was back.

"I can't talk to her about this. But there's a big dent in the back of the thing, above the extra tire. I put it there myself, with the side of an axe, after chopping firewood one night in Idaho."

Pletch looked at me like he thought I might tell Jimmy Tim Morton what I knew. For a harmless looking, thin old man with a hawk nose and nostrils so narrow it looked like he couldn't breathe in any air, Pletch was menacing.

"I guess camping's not right for you. But it's good

to find out before you buy one of those things yourself."

"Young man, I'm a retired accountant. I've had a life of some distinction. And now I'm sneaking around beating up on my neighbor's RV. I'll never recover from this trip."

Ethel took him to Memorial Hospital at 11:00. I got Delbert Simmons to come out of Harbor Side, where he usually stopped for a coffee before midnight. Delbert offered to drive them in his black and white. He wouldn't have done that unless he saw this as an emergency.

I thought it was a good plan, since the sight of his Airstream was liable to kill Pletch for sure. But Ethel wanted to drive.

Delbert adjusted the band on his Mariners baseball cap, expanding it a half size. The late night caffeine, or perhaps the sudden intrusion of a potential crisis, must have puffed his cranium. He was using a toothpick to clean wax from his drooping ears.

"I'll lead the way," he offered, "since you won't let me chauffeur. Or would you go for an ambulance?"

"It's not that serious," she said. "I wouldn't want to scare papa."

They stood in my office discussing alternatives while Pletch sat gasping on the recliner. The old man kept saying nothing hurt.

"We wait any longer," Delbert said, looking at Pletch, "and he may go from queasy to critical."

Delbert led the way, lights flashing, and I watched the Airstream jounce out onto the road. By 2:00, when I was ready to leave for the apartment, Ethel was back alone.

"They couldn't get him stabilized," was all she said. She went back to their room.

Pletch went home in a coffin that looked like a mini-Airstream. I never understood why Ethel picked that one over the wooden boxes, although she maintained Enos didn't really mind the Airstream as much as he said.

***

The family that came in this evening in their green Ford wagon—the Franklin Welches from Columbus, Ohio—was very bedraggled, a perfect example of the species. I could tell they fought the motel option all vacation and that Pilgrim's Harbor represented defeat. They'd said they were going to camp every night, but here they were.

The only explanation I can offer for my kindness to the Welches was the impact of my day with Cindy Bonds. I was nice to the Welches, I was empathetic, and I was patient. Mellow would be the word. This is a family I would normally have toyed with like a cat with yarn.

The Welches sat in their wagon for five full minutes, the motor off, before Franklin slowly emerged and tromped into the office. He was making the gestures associated with straightening one's tie although all he had on was an old tee-shirt.

For a small man, he moved big. His left arm, from about mid-biceps to wrist, was burned bright red from being stuck out the window all day.

"What's a room?"

One of those, I thought. "Twenty-eight fifty for two twins, plus the kids will be four each. Also plus tax."

"How about if the kids sleep on the floor, in their bags?"

"That's what I meant. Cots are extra."

"Could you see your way clear to $26, all told?"
"$26 all told?"
"We'd use our own towels, our own glasses."
Welch was very polite, sweating as if right off the trail, smelling a little loamy. Maybe one of the kids had dumped a fist of dirt on dad's head. Just what I needed.
"The ten and a half matters a lot?"
"We've been gone a week longer than I planned. I'll probably be spending my raise as it is."
"Where do you work?"
It was an unusual question to ask before the registration card was filled out. But this was an unusual situation.
"Batelle. Consulting."
Then something clicked. I remembered playing with a toy when I was a kid, a kind of miniature pinball machine on stumpy legs that made all sorts of noises. It sounded like Welch's firm might manufacture them.
The idea of toys makes me feel sentimental. Although it's always best to play it safe with the guests, I decided to help the poor man out. After all, the guy worked to make kids happy.
"Twenty six bucks then."
I gave him #12. Everything worked.
It made me feel satisfied. I could see the kids carry in the sleeping bags, Mrs. Welch dump the melted ice from their blue plastic cooler, and Franklin pore over his maps on the hood of the Ford. Dewey's Good Deed.

***

Never, not once, did I stay in a motel when I was a kid. Despite all the traveling we did, and all the times we drove the highways for one or another relocation, motels were simply not our way.

It's hard for me to believe now. But then, I didn't even know it was an option.

Some of the times, we stayed with friends. Or rather, with what my parents called friends. I'd call them passing acquaintances, at best. It was frequently embarrassing. They might even be friends of friends, distant cousins, people who once worked for the same outfit my father once worked for, though not necessarily at the same time.

We'd just drop in and hope to stay the night. Often as not, these friends didn't know my parents on sight. I learned to recognize the look in their faces that said *who?* But my parents were experts at conviviality and could usually get us lodged.

Some other times, we just slept in the car at the side of the road. If it was summery, we might have a couple of blankets and find a safe place to sleep off the road. We did the Rest Stop circuit. I'd never heard of National Parks.

Several times my father got jobs with hotels in small cities. He worked as a bellhop, parking attendant, helper in kitchens, whatever. I'd been to a few, when he'd let me visit his "office." When I first heard people talking about a motel, I just assumed they were mispronouncing hotel.

***

Roscoe Pompers was blind. He came into the office wearing wire-rimmed sunglasses at about 9:30, led by a white German shepherd. I didn't hear a car pull up.

"Any rooms?" he asked. "I didn't see if your No Vacancy sign was on."

"Two left. You're in luck."

He reached out a gloved right hand. I didn't know if he wanted a handshake or the registration material, so for a moment I did nothing.

"Come on, fella," he said, wiggling his fingers. "Let me get signed up before someone comes along and takes my room."

"You need some help with the writing?"

"I need help, I'll ask. Gimme a pen, put an index card at the line where you want me to sign, and back off."

After he'd registered, Pompers dropped the pen on the floor and stuck out his hand again. The dog picked the pen up in its mouth. She began chewing it like a chicken bone.

"I need a little more information, Mr. Pompers."

"Like what?"

"Home address, phone, that sort of thing. Car type and license number."

"Jesus Christ, I'm just staying the night, not taking out a mortgage."

"That's all right, then. What about parking?"

"None required."

"Room 57. Third from the end on your left."

"I'll find it."

"Here, let me help you with the door."

The dog snarled at me as if offended by my offer. She'd obviously picked up the cues from her master.

"I want your help, I'll ask for it. Already told you that."

"It's all right. I don't mind helping you to the room."

"No it ain't all right, Goddamn it." He headed for the door, groped for the knob, and flung it open. "Let's go, Hilde," he barked at the dog.

I still heard no car. Rather than ask him anything else, I decided not to worry about how he'd gotten here or how he'd leave in the morning.

***

I've been dreaming more lately than I have in years. Vivid, technicolor dreams, none of them nightmares but many of them leaving me terrified when I awaken. So the good dreams are most welcomed.

Tonight, I didn't exactly dream about Cindy Bonds. I had my typical midwest-period dream, the one in which a woman walks out of my apartment carrying two suitcases, gets in her car, and drives off with her tail lights gaining rather than lessening in intensity. Then their red aura bursts into holocaustal white light and it becomes clear that another woman is arriving, her headlights sweeping over the parking lot. I walk out to meet her, carrying her two suitcases into my apartment, unable to see the details of her face because of the darkness. As she turns to greet me, I always awake before having the chance to know who she is.

Tonight, though, I hung on long enough to see that the woman who arrives could be Cindy. Nothing ruled her out. Same color hair, same shape, the pearl earrings. But the woman in my dream had no eyes, at least none that I could see in the instant before I awoke.

CHAPTER ELEVEN

The crab's got Lou Pumphrey. Stomach. They say he's already thrown away the china his wife left him. Eats only cold food out of its container.

I'm sorry to see this happen to a guy like Lou. It makes me want to be easier on Jennifer. But I'm sure The Pumph wouldn't be above using sympathy to get a few extra days off. Have to be careful.

Lou had run the Eagle's Aerie Inn west of Pilgrim's Harbor for over twenty years and left it when he got sick the first time. That was when I hired Lou's daughter, hoping Jennifer might also have the business in her blood.

Maybe she won't get cancer, either.

The doctor thought he'd cut it all out. So Lou bought into a little place in town serving Continental cuisine. Lou in his restaurant was like Casey Stengel trying to coach soccer at Yale.

It had a dark bar and no more than a dozen tables, very classy for the area. Lou renamed it Henri's and tried to get the locals to pronounce it fancy: "On-Reez." They kept calling it Henry's, though, with a heavy emphasis on the Hen.

To get on Lou's nerves, close friends called the restaurant Hank's. That was the name his partner went by anyway. Keeping Lou frustrated had become local sport, retaliation for all those years his athletic talent frustrated his friends.

Cancer was all Lou talked about after his first operation.

He wouldn't put crab on the menu, no dishes with ham or bacon, no sodas with saccharine. When the country watched Hubert Humphrey die in '78, the experience changed Lou permanently. He'd stomp around Henri's, going from table to table with a snifter of Christian Brothers brandy in his thick fist because he believed in its medicinal properties, and complain about the media coverage.

"Why don't they stop? There's got to be pictures of him from before the C."

He'd turn around and find another set of diners. "They ought to play all his old speeches and forget about now."

At the next table, he'd wave his arms and point toward Minnesota. "You see what he looked like? Neck's going to break off trying to hold up his head."

They say Lou has six months. He used to be a rock and now he's just remains. Won't let anyone help him except his daughter, who's staying home by him like she says.

The bad thing is that after she found the cock on the bed in #43, the Pumph went into a real tailspin. It happened on my day off. I'd have loved to see it, although I'm sorry it had to happen now.

Guests often leave things behind in the beds. Paperbacks and bowls of Triscuits, socks, wine bottles. Alla Mae has the Pilgrim's Harbor record for total dollar value of items found, although Alla Mae's cousin Anna Mae set the single item record with a diamond pendant she almost threw away as a worthless trinket. There've been pipes, decks of cards, alarm clocks, ankle bracelets, diaries, baseball gloves. I usually forward the lost items to their owners.

What the Pumph found early on the 25th got written on the report as a marital device. Good old Alla Mae. It was molded rubber, shaped like the real thing, though a good eight inches long, and carefully detailed. Veins, a slight bend toward the end, a little hole carved into the tip. It turned on with a switch where the balls should be and then began to purr and twitch.

I heard that when the Pumph began to strip the bed and found it between the sheets, she panicked. She thought it was the genuine article. A woman named Diane January stayed in #43 the night before. She probably fell asleep using the thing and forgot to pack it in the morning.

The whole matter disturbs me. It forces me to realize how little I know about dealing intimately with women compared with what I know about dealing with strangers.

I don't know what to do with it. Throwing it in the trash seems like the kind of thing that brings a man bad luck. But I can't see mailing it to Ms. January. I have it wrapped in yesterday's *Courier* like a pike fillet and stashed in the trunk of my Pinto for now.

Walking back to my office, I tried to imagine how the Pumph would explain to her father why she was so upset. Lou Pumphrey was famous for his patience and equally famous for losing it when his daughter was hurt or sad. Then look out. He'd actually spanked a boy when the Pumph was in fourth grade and had come home crying about yanked pigtails. Pretty as she was, the Pumph had trouble getting dates in high school because of Lou.

Lou was also famous for his notorious baseball career. He pitched in the St. Louis Browns organization during World War II, when they had a one-armed outfielder and a bunch of 35-year-old rookies. Men who couldn't serve in the armed forces. Lou didn't make it to the majors, even under those circumstances.

His hometown friends kidded him about it—his great gifts, his tools, his talent, how he couldn't run fast, but it didn't matter since he couldn't hit. He was a star in semi-pro, though, before and after his career with the Browns.

I refuse to think of Lou as a loser. The way I look at

it, Lou's ledger sheet might not balance, but at least he had a good number of entries on the credit side. Sometimes I wonder if the same can be said about me, unless you really weighted good health three or four times over anything else.

I chipped in to buy Lou a comfortable chair, a real leather recliner to help make the last months more pleasant. It's important to be part of the community where you work.

***

A man came in and asked if I minded whether he sold art out front by the entrance. It would just be for one night and he promised not to be pushy. He would lean his work against the outside wall of the office and stay clear of the walkway.

I want to support the arts. All my coffee cups come from summer art fairs. Who knows, I may even try to sell my carvings some day. So I agreed.

Then I saw the work. It shouldn't take an M.B.A. to know you see the merchandise before you agree to display it.

I know a little about painting. There's *Addie, Woman in Black*, which reminds me of my mother. There's Andrew Wyeth. If I ever wrote my memoirs, Edward Hopper's *Western Motel* would be on the cover. I know enough to know this Lorenzo Hegan's painting is outrageous.

It isn't a question of taste, either. Hegan took black velvet painting down to its next logical level.

His canvases were styrofoam, large chunks hacked from the sides of picnic coolers. His medium appeared to be enamel house paint, which was slathered on with foot-wide brushes. And his theme was the reclining male figure, or as much as could be suggested by a half dozen strokes of the thick brush.

There was no mistaking that the figures were meant to be male, nor on which side the figures were reclining. Behind each figure was a glob of yellow, red, or orange, probably to suggest the sun at different times of the day. Each had been sprayed with a lacquer-like coating that gleamed in the sun.

At least Hegan didn't sell anything. He left at dark. I can't swear that the paintings cost me guests, but more cars than usual drove back onto the Interstate after stopping to look at the outside of Pilgrim's Harbor.

Just before Hegan left, he gave me a painting for the wall. Morning, with the man lying on his left side.

"Thanks for the support," he said. "Hang this up over the cigarette machine and get rid of that silly gnome you've got standing there."

CHAPTER TWELVE

Finfer finally called. It was late, so I had time to sit and talk without interruptions from guests.

It was like hearing from an old pal. I average about two personal calls a year at Pilgrim's Harbor.

"I hear you've been working your way through the Woonsocket phone book trying to find me."

"Only three major calls. City Hall, Willis Cowley, and your sister."

"Not exactly a cross section of the voting public of The Ocean State, but I appreciate your effort. Let me send you a check for the expense."

"No need. Consider it my contribution to the campaign." I was smiling as I spoke. Having fun on the phone was an uncommon experience.

"I didn't realize the briefcase was gone until Syracuse. Then I had no idea where it was. Reviewed my itinerary and saw myself carrying it out of your place, clear as a yes-vote."

"That just shows how badly you need these notes and things you left behind. We wouldn't want the campaign to hinge on that memory of yours."

"I was wondering about something. Have you read through it all?"

"No, no. I just glanced at it trying to see how much of an emergency we have here."

"Good. I suppose a lot of it ought to be confidential."

I heard the edge in Finfer's voice. Was he worried I would leak something to the press? Hell, I don't know what Finfer's pile of notes means. I don't know anyone in the media or how things get leaked. I operate in a different sort of world.

"Where do you want it sent," I asked, "and how?"

"Well now, I'm working on that. A student of mine, Jay Ladue, is driving east for the summer to help in the campaign. If I find him in time, maybe he can stop at your place and pick it up."

"Don't you need it sooner than that? I mean, it must be valuable stuff."

"Sometimes, the most valuable stuff is best left out of reach."

I felt much better talking to Finfer in person. On the phone, without seeing how he stood and whether he smiled, everything became innuendo.

This was now the first phone call lasting over three minutes that I'd had in months. Maybe I was simply out of practice.

"I can try to keep it safe. But as I told your sister, it's not like I've got a vault here to keep it in."

"Understood. But I've seen how you operate and I'll take my chances. Hope it works out, because this kid, Ladue, is good company. You'll like talking to him and you can always use the business. Is it settled?"

"Do you get a referral fee?"

"It's the least I can do, after all you've done for me. I'll let you know if and when to expect him."

I understood that Finfer was being charming. But I didn't like it.

This Finfer and the Finfer from a few days ago at Pilgrim's Harbor were not the same. It shows the risk of knowing someone a few minutes past the proper time for goodbye.

Maybe Finfer was simply taking himself and his mission more seriously now that he'd reached Rhode Island. Besides, it was very late in the east.

As if practicing, he continued to chat. I wondered if he recalled what I look like.

"Let me tell you a great story."

"It's your nickel."

I sat back, shifted the phone to my other ear, and shut my eyes. Enjoying phone conversations requires a real effort.

"The lousiest job working for a politician is speechwriter," Finfer said.

"Advance man sounded worse to me. I see them here once in a while, in a sweat, sleeves rolled up and ties at half-mast. They all move around like squirrels; they're skinny and eat nuts."

Finfer didn't seem to be listening. When I stopped speaking, he was part-way through another sentence.

"... really read the speeches, see, they all just wing it."

I waited. I wasn't sure if I was supposed to speak.

"How can you tell?"

"Well, when they're reading, they get lost sometimes and look down to find their places. When they wing it, they get lost too but just keep going. There's lots of *ands*."

"Nixon. He read those last speeches on tv, didn't he?"

"I wasn't counting him. He wasn't a real live politician anymore by then."

"So what are you telling me? You're going to be Elizabeth Mack Cowley's speechwriter?"

"No, I met this guy who used to write speeches for Richard Daley. You ever hear of him? Chicago. We've got his speechwriter out here as a consultant. He told me about writing for Daley and handed me a transcript of one of his last speeches. Verbatim, the way Daley said it in front of the state legislature. Got it right here."

Finfer rattled some papers, muttered a few words and cleared his throat.

"You need to hear this," he said. "In toto."

He was actually going to read the speech. At least the telephone rates were lower at this hour. There were worse ways for me to spend the time between final check-in and going home.

"'A few years ago,'" Finfer said in what were intended to be stentorian tones, "'I visited the great and renounced Speaker, Sam Rayburn, in his offers in the House of Representatives. And I say to you as I know men and women on both sides of this aisle will agree, no greater American ever served in the Congress of the United States as Sam Rayburn. He reminded me on the day I met him, in '56, his first speech to the floor in the Congress, and I'm repeating what he said.

"'He said there is no north, there is no south, there is no east and there is no west. We're all American and we should approach the question of our country and that basis.

"'And I say to you today, on behalf of the lame and the crippled and the handicapped citizens and children of Chicago and Illinois, God love them, and I say to you today in the hollowed halls of this chambers: there's no north and south, there's no east and west in this state. We're all members and citizens of a great state and that's the way it should always be.'"

Somebody laughed uproariously behind Finfer, who began giggling. I thought he'd sounded sober.

"Is that it?" I asked.

I hear insider's stories all the time—bull semen stories, aluminum siding stories, the right time to mix a martini with sweet vermouth stories—but it was difficult to know how to respond over the phone.

"I'm telling you," Finfer said when he'd calmed himself, "Daley must have had them mesmerized."

"With that?"

"Nah, it's all personality, see. He's asking for a quarter of a billion dollars for his city's schools, and this speechwriter has all kinds of dollar figures and population stuff in his speech, and Daley doesn't use any of it."

"Too bad."

"You're missing my point." Finfer's voice held its good nature and charm, the teacher turned campaigner had high style. But there was a hint of leaning forward and pointing at me in the voice. "Don't you see? You're like this speechwriter guy."

Suddenly, I felt disconnected, as if my jack had been yanked from the plug and only the phone was working properly. I had no sense of what Finfer was talking about.

"Come again?" Finfer had me off safe ground.

"You create a place for people to take off from there at your motel. You have a place they can land when their productive time starts to end. We all need that, though we don't like to think about it."

There was a pause. I tried to speak, but only managed a faint exhale. Too bad Finfer couldn't see me nodding. Phones aren't good for anything except reservations.

"Let me think about that one."

"I've been thinking about it all trip. Staying in these damn motels. A lot of people fill that spot, that landing place, in other people's lives. You follow me?"

"Maybe. I guess my view is smaller. One little night of peace."

"Give yourself more credit. The heights of serendipity are best reached when a person knows he's got a decent place to stay the night and a solid speech to fall back on when he loses the inspiration."

I couldn't follow him. I liked what Finfer seemed to be saying, but I wasn't sure he was saying what he seemed to be saying. I needed to bring him down to reality, my reality.

"Mr. Finfer, a guy can go without food longer than he can without rest. That's my trade. They can make of it what they want."

"I suppose."

But I could tell Finfer was gone. He'd given his lecture and was putting his things away; the bell had rung.

We recapped the plan for his briefcase and said we'd speak again soon, after Finfer reached Jay Ladue. I held the receiver in my hand afterwards, listening to the high whine reminding me to hang up.

Finfer didn't understand that connections do get made in my business. Transient, superficial, but part of a service. It might be nice if I offered something more permanent to my guests, like Finfer was saying, but that was unrealistic.

In my opinion, for guests at Pilgrim's Harbor the only thing that's permanent is the road.

When Finfer calls back, I'll get him to clarify. But I knew Finfer wouldn't remember what he'd said tonight.

That was one trouble with intimate conversations across 2,000 miles. They had a tendency to be out of control, too filtered by distance to work the way you wanted them to work. The old face-to-face is the only system for Dewey Howser.

CHAPTER THIRTEEN

I had a heart-to-heart today with Alla Mae. That's a face-to-face cubed, Palaver Grande. She was leaving Pilgrim's Harbor just as I arrived.

Alla Mae's last name is Buhl, but she's one of those people you never think of by last name. It might be because of her two part given name, or the fit between her name and personality, or the sufficiency of simply calling her Alla Mae. But I'm certain no one else at Pilgrim's Harbor knows she's Buhl.

Unlike nearly everyone I know, Alla Mae could not be from anywhere else. Her appearance at first suggests vast experience of the world and wide-ranging wisdom. But on closer observation, it's clear that the wreath of seasoning which surrounds her is actually empirical pessimism. It isn't that she's seen it all, just that she's seen enough.

With her wide resigned face, bulging brow, and heavy heart, a man might have admired her when she was young. But he wouldn't have lusted after her. She's twice-married and childless, the best employee I have.

From the first, Alla Mae accepted me as necessary and hasn't been inclined to get any closer. She runs a notch shy of cordial and well above rude. Her vocabulary is light on adjectives and her sentences range from incomplete to terse.

There's nothing personal in Alla Mae's relations with people. For her, people seem to be what comes along with the Big Sky, like clouds, arbitrarily placed and not very significant in the scheme of things. The only part of the hospitality industry she can tolerate is maid service. Anonymity is fine with her.

I think this is why her eyes go skyward if I talk to her too long. She listens, takes it all in and keeps careful records, but she never lets me know what she thinks. As a consequence, I feel like a tolerated toddler when I talk to her.

Alla Mae is sixty and hasn't missed work since the Klover Korner Motel became Pilgrim's Harbor. But from the set of her jaw all June, I could tell that something had been nettling her. I felt it was time to ask. So I held the door to my office open for her and she shouldered past me with a grunt.

"Nothing," she answered.

"Well, you just don't seem yourself lately, is all."

"Am, though."

"Your arthritis acting up?"

"Never doesn't."

I couldn't get her to sit despite pointing to chairs, sitting on my desk, gesturing at the bench. She kept shaking out her rag, which looked like the back section of a Pendleton shirt. She folded it into a tight square, but wouldn't budge.

"OK, I just thought maybe there was something and we could talk."

Getting out the Scotch was a stroke of genius. I produced it for her with a flourish, a rabbit from the hat.

"Lord, look at that," she said. A smile threatened at the lower right edge of her mouth, but you had to be looking to see it.

I held the pint to the light and swirled it so she could hear it was still half full. The glasses beneath my counter were not yet dirty enough to justify washing, so I dusted them against my shirt and set them on the blotter.

"How do you take it?"

"Neat."

She plopped in the chair and sank, resting her head on its hard back. I wondered if she was going to kick off her shoes, the transformation was that dramatic.

Alla Mae swilled her shot and thrust the glass out to me. While mine lingered in its ice and water, she gripped the second in her lap, breathing deeply.

"Guest left this for me a couple days ago."

She nodded. I never noticed how thin Alla Mae's hair is now, a lush brown shag gone threadbare, nor how spotted the skin around her brow has become. She's been such a steady worker that I failed to consider her age.

"That's what I mean," she said.

When her logic is hardest to follow, Alla Mae's usually on the verge of a real breakthrough. So I sipped and took a chip of ice to chew. Scotch at two is not my custom.

"What's what you mean?"

"None of these kids would leave you nothing," she said. "No give, only take."

There were three good shots left. I handed her the bottle and put my feet up. Nobody would be checking in for an hour or so.

"I know what you mean."

"You don't. But do a round of rooms with one of them and you would. Kids."

"Things come too easy for them nowadays."

"That ain't it. No one's around long enough anymore to cover the big stuff for the kids, tell them things. Everybody's out working, off gallivanting, whatever. You want the wheat to grow, you've got to control the weeds. Nothing's got any structure anymore."

It was the longest speech I'd heard her make in years. But I still wasn't sure if something specific was bothering her or if this was just random rancor.

"Let any of them off the Fourth," she said, "and you ought to go back to manager school. That's all I got to say."

I leaned forward, a counterthrust to the blow. So that was it.

"Alla Mae, the Fourth's a tough one."

"No tougher than deciding whether to let a baby suck teat every hour. It's your milk, you set up the schedule."

With that, she gulped the last of her drink and stood. She looked at me directly, maybe two tenths of a second less than a glower, and then left with growled thanks.

I agree with Alla Mae in principle. I can't possibly give all the kids off the Fourth. But the staff is entitled to a day off a month and I have to be reasonable.

Like a guest from Detroit once told me, the guy who

ought to be tenor in the quartet is the guy who can sing tenor.

I'll only give Jennifer Pumphrey the day off. With her father dying and all she's been through, you can call it extenuating circumstances. But it worries me that Alla Mae might think I'd blown it.

***

Elliott Courtenay checked in about 6:30. He's my June writer. It was getting close—I almost never get through a whole month without at least one person telling me he's a writer. Here it is June the 28th; had me worried. I've seen this particular sort of writer many times. Travels solo, but he's got his typewriter in the front seat with him like a passenger and there are boxes of books in back. Does the colony circuit, California to Wyoming to upstate New York, and then retires for six months to a trailer court in Florida. Always working on a dozen projects, eking out his gas and meal money.

"Working on a travel piece?" I asked.

"Kinda. I'm collecting data and I'll write when it's all over, whenever and wherever that may be."

"Sounds like a mystery book to me."

"I'm doing a project that's sponsored by the National Endowment," he said sadly, as if I'd mind that he has some of my tax money. "It's a book on how communities all over America celebrated the Bicentennial. It only covers towns older than 100 years and having fewer than 500 inhabitants."

I nodded. He held up the key as if hoping to see through it.

"Sounded like a good idea when I first proposed it,"

he continued. "Took a while to get funded, then a while more to get started. Now nobody remembers much about how they celebrated the Bicentennial. I'm having trouble with the raw materials."

As soon as Courtenay left for his room, an Adam's apple walked in followed by its lanky owner. The Adam's apple bobbled and the man smiled.

"Hope you can make me happier than you made that guy."

There are times when having to switch from sadly compassionate to instantly jovial is a strain. I smiled at this new guest, Howard Mermel from Hartford.

"That'll take more than I can offer him here," was the best I could manage.

"Me and the mizz would like your bridal suite."

"Which one, the three room or the four room suite?"

"I can see you have a sense of humor. I can also see you need to have your teeth worked on." He gave me his card. Dr. Howard Mermel, D.D.S. "That front left is badly discolored. What'd you do, dive into an empty pool? But seriously, what you want to shop around for—you do have dentists out here, don't you?—is called bonding. Room for two, please. With access to the veranda."

It was all I could do to keep from telling him we were full. What you want to shop around for is The Shady Rest Motel a day's drive south of here.

"You'll have to take the river view. Veranda side always goes by 6:00."

"If we ever reach Nevada, the mizz and me are planning to be married. Unfortunately, we seem to have lost our way. Isn't Nevada back that way?"

I wish Cindy Bonds would declare herself reachable.

***

I sat alone in my office. The weather had turned suddenly hot, as it always does in late June the day before the natives say "hey, doesn't it know this is summer?" The flow of guests was subsiding for the night. We were half full.

Maybe it was tonight's duller crowd, or Alla Mae's tone this afternoon. Maybe it was the shift in temperature, or the time of day. Something in this particular day reminded me of my childhood. It wasn't an unpleasant sensation, but it was gnawing at me.

The stages of my life are neat: childhood in the east, adolescence in the midwest, adulthood in the west. My memories seldom cross over the mountains or rivers that separate them.

It's an understatement to say we often relocated when I was young. I can still remember my mother crying on the porch in Brainerd, Minnesota—no, it was Lancaster, Pennsylvania—when my father said we were leaving again. That had to be when I was no more than seven or eight.

She had become attached to the bungalow we rented. There was a little garden for the first time—cucumbers, peppers, tomatoes, zucchini—and a shed for her digging tools. It never got as hot as Florida had, never as cold as Maine.

My father, Stu Howser, was working in the cigar factory and had done well for a time. I remember that the city smelled of tobacco leaves. In the mornings, when he would kiss me goodbye and grub a spoonful of Rice Krinkles, his shirt already smelled like a box of panatellas.

"I'm on the wagon, Lucy," he would brag.

"This is a nice little town," she would answer.

But it didn't last. This time—Lancaster—when he told

her he'd been fired again, my mother was much more upset than ever before.

"Oh, Stuart, this just didn't have to happen."

He squatted next to where she sat on the top step, one huge mitt on her shoulder. His arms were flecked with gray like ashes and his hair had become the color of smoke.

"There's jobs in Virginia," he said.

It never occurred to me before that their marriage might not be good. She went where he went, her mood ranging from stoic to hopeful, and she set up a home. Lucy and Stuart, Lu and Stu, the Howsers from here and there. That day was when I realized she might not be happy.

I loved to see them dance the Virginia Reel, which must have been back in Lee County, South Carolina, during the cotton year. Their hands were up and touching to form a bridge that friends passed under, Lu on her tip-toes and Stu hunched over so he wouldn't be unreachable. That was the essence of connection, love as it ought to be in the eyes of a child.

On the porch in Lancaster, when Stuart told her it was time to move on, it became clear to me how often and how deeply my father hurt my mother. His tenderness was no help.

"Doo-wee-doo," she moaned. That was her call for me and I always came when she made it. "Doo-wee-doo, time to round up the boxes." Tears curved past her cheekbones and down her chin like glue for a stage-beard.

"I don't want to leave," I said. I meant Lancaster, but my mother misunderstood.

"I'll be all right now. Go behind the grocery store and find us some nice strong boxes. With tops."

"We've got plenty in the closets," my father said. "The boy doesn't have to run out if he doesn't want to."

"We need more now."

I backed down the stairs, watching them watch me without really seeing. I heard her say, "twelve times now in sixteen years together." My father must have squeezed her shoulder hard because she tucked it toward her chest in a half-shrug.

So we moved near Lynchburg and he cut tobacco instead of folding it. Somewhere on Long Island, truck farming. Janitor work in an office complex, Rye, New York. I used to say my childhood ended in a New Jersey city that smelled of meat.

After a while, we moved to Brainerd, Minnesota, and my father worked in a papermill. Paul Bunyan's hometown. He did cereal in Cedar Rapids, potato processing in Grand Forks, fruit in Traverse City. I'm leaving some out.

I don't know where my father heard about the jobs, but the man never had trouble finding work. Just keeping it.

He died in Milwaukee of a cerebral hemorrhage. Was gone by the time I reached the hospital from school, before Lucy had finished her first coffee in the waiting room. When I arrived, she was sitting there blowing at the steam rising from the cup.

I was sixteen. My mother, not yet forty, looked older than the woman fighting gout who sat beside her telling people she was sixty-two and never sick a day in her life.

"He got to work," my mother said, "changed, closed his locker, stood up to put on his helmet, and fell over. That Claude Crandall he's been pals with thought Stu conked himself with the hard-hat."

"Did you see him?"

"Nothing to see. He was all but gone." She looked at me and her face began to tremble. "He wouldn't have known me or anything."

I saw her sad eyes and could not distinguish a difference between them then and when I'd left home after breakfast that morning. What I started to say to her wouldn't have mattered, so I stopped after "That's . . ."

"Right," she said. "That's par for the course."

After the funeral, I just stopped going to school. There hadn't been much continuity in my education anyway. I could start eleventh grade someplace else, some other time.

"What do you want to do?" my mother asked.

"Get a job."

"Let me do that first. I have this urge to be a bus driver."

She did, and stayed on after I went back to school, graduated, and moved down to Chicago. I had enough credits at various colleges in and around the city to risk adorning myself with a B.A., for all the checking up anyone would do once I left the area. I got together with my mother from time to time and, although she promised to, she never did take me for a joyride on one of her buses.

Not long after that, I headed west. My mother died four years ago and all I kept was one snapshot of her in uniform, smiling as I never saw her smile with my father. Jaunty little angle to the cap, gleam off the badge, and a bowling glove on her left hand to help with the turns.

***

I understand what brings these memories back. You take Alla Mae talking about give-and-take, the Pumph and her dying father, these people coming to Pilgrim's Harbor day after day, and you mix it in with a jigger of loneliness and a pinch of hope (Cindy Bonds). Shake well and keep in the back room until ready to serve.

The interlude of reminiscence was interrupted at 10:30 by the noisy arrival of a beat-up Volkswagen bug. It idled beneath the carport, which intensified the racket. I walked to the window to preview what was coming.

In the harsh light, I could see through the rear window that the backseat was filled with running shoes. There had to be hundreds of them and they were stuffed in there, not just heaped. Every imaginable color, all sorts of brands, and all used to within their last possible mile.

Out popped a small man in running shorts and tee shirt, wearing a pink and green cap with its bill up, and with both knees taped. It was 10:30 at night, but the guy looked ready for a race. He scooted past me into the office and bowed when I shut the door behind him.

His name was Dolfy Toskol. He wore frameless glasses, a neatly trimmed beard with matching coins of gray on each side of his chin, and a watch that beeped every few seconds.

"This is great," he said.

"Glad you like the place."

"No. I mean, it's probably fine, but I was talking about something else. Do you know what it says on my odometer?"

"Er, . . ."

"Exactly 112,000 miles. Isn't that great?"

"Those bugs sure last. Here, why don't you sign the

registration form. I'm sure you're tired."

"I never get tired. Listen to me: I bought that thing when it had 102,000 miles on it exactly. We're talking 10,000 miles—on the nose—in four years. I'm still ahead."

He began to fill out the form, but stopped after each entry to continue talking. He probably couldn't talk and deal with the form at the same time because of how his tongue stuck out of the corner of his mouth when he wrote.

"The goal is to run more miles before I die than the car does before it dies. Starting four years ago, of course. As of today, I've got 10,101 to the Bug's 10,000. But I had these knee problems this year.

"What I've been doing is driving maybe 15, 20 miles a day since spring. Then I stop and run 10 or 12 myself. Pretty soon, I'll be back up to normal mileage and the Bug won't have caught me.

"It's getting close, though. I have to be in San Francisco to give a speech in September."

He handed me the form. In the space for his address, Toskol had put his license plate number. There was no phone number and no credit card information. He'd pay cash.

"I figure the car's got another 30,000 left, max. Me too, at the rate I run. That's twelve years. No male in my family ever lived past 53 anyhow."

I gave him #41, for good luck. At about 11:00, I saw him take off down the road, running toward town.

CHAPTER FOURTEEN

I was at the office by 1:30. If there's going to be a party on the Fourth of July, a week away, then I have plans to make. Especially since I'll be short one maid.

When Cindy called, I had just finished checklisting the rooms and authorizing the Pumph and her cohorts to leave for the day. For some reason, Dolfy Toskol in #41 hadn't checked out.

I didn't worry about that yet. The workday was beginning to be too unpredictable for my tastes. I hoped, but hadn't expected, to hear from Cindy before the end of the month.

"This isn't a real call," she said. "I just need a favor from you."

"Just remember that the Harbor Side doesn't carry vegetarian Gainesburgers."

"I can't believe I moved into a place with no plants. It's positively unwholesome. I didn't get any sleep last night."

"It wasn't a big night for me either. You should have called."

"Must get to a nursery. Today."

"But I can't leave here."

It was more a complaint than a turndown. Ready as I was to be with Cindy, I wasn't ready to shirk responsibility at Pilgrim's Harbor. Nothing could get in the way of my work commitment.

"I know. That's why I called."

Outside, framed by the front window, the Pumph waved from the driver's seat of her Impala. I gave her the OK sign, already as dizzied by Cindy as I'd been inside the pet store. I stared as the car sped off spewing gravel.

It was a sunny afternoon. That fact registered in the space vacated by the Pumph's Impala. A breeze shook the trees. There was a strong banana smell in the office, like the smell in the kitchen when my mother decided to bake banana bread because I'd let all the bananas turn black. Someone must have tossed a peel in my wastebasket while he was checking out.

"We could start this conversation again," I said. "Good afternoon, Pilgrim's Harbor."

"I know you're busy. I know you can't leave. That's why I called."

"You're losing me again."

"I've got my bike assembled."

"Oh."

"What I'd like to do is ride my bike out to the motel and borrow your car. I can get to the nursery, take a load of plants back here, return your car, and bike home. Simple. I'd be done before you needed the car to go home tonight."

"You mean you won't stop in and say hello?"

"You'll be busy. Besides, I'm not reachable yet."

There was no point in being difficult. It would be better to wait until Cindy was ready. But I hated to let her go again.

"It's a deal," I said. "I'll leave the key behind the driver's sun visor."

"Very crafty."

"My guess is you'll stock up on rhodies."

"Some. But I don't go with just one species. Remember that. Saxifrage to Swedish ivy, and no kitchen is complete without a philodendron."

"Speaking of which, the Pinto's clutch is a little stiff. And you have to turn the directional signal off with your hand."

"I'll manage."

She hung up before I could respond. Cindy used neither hello nor goodbye in her conversations.

I can't remember the last time I let someone drive my car. This business makes you a stickler on insurance. But it didn't faze me with Cindy.

She'd be a careful driver, since adeptness and self-reliance were major components of her act. Besides, if there were an accident, she'd probably be nice when contrite.

***

Dolfy Toskol had a plan. He appeared in the office after Cindy had hung up.

"Fourth of July's coming, you know," he said.

"I heard."

"What this town needs on the Fourth is a road race. The Run for Freedom 10K, or the Independence Day Classic, something like that. You have a lot of runners?"

There was something about Toskol's enthusiasm that put me off. My reaction probably wasn't very fair, though, because he seemed like a nice man. Just obsessed.

"The boom hasn't come this way yet."

"Sure it has. Had to. You probably don't notice them, is all. Cooped up in here all the time. But we'd better make it a 5K, just in case. Anybody can run 3.1 miles, right?"

"In how many days?"

"I love it!" Toskol shouted. "The holiday's five days away, you know that."

I looked at him closely. Yup, he actually didn't get it. "So what're you going to do, stay here for five days for some kind of race?"

"Sure, you've got room. I can get fifty, sixty miles ahead of the car this way. And I can finally run in a race that I have a chance of winning! I've always wanted to race somewhere that there aren't too many fast guys, too many hard-core runners. If I can do 5K in 18 flat, I might win the whole thing."

Then he took out a pad and began to jot down notes. He'd have to print up race announcements and entry forms fast. He'd have to mark out a course, talk to the police about traffic control, see if he could get medical people to stand by, arrange for water and people who'd stay along the course to hand it out, test his timer, find somebody to donate trophies.

"You know anybody in the media?" he asked.

"There isn't much media here. *The Courier* and KUTE-AM radio, that's about it."

"It's a small place. I'll do it word-of-mouth. I can run the whole town in a day."

CHAPTER FIFTEEN

The last time I had black guests was a year ago August. Ty Johnson and his daughter Renee. Johnson had been taking his daughter and a U-Haul of belongings to Stanford.

Today, Wes Tripplett checked in at 4:30. He had the biggest Afro I've ever seen. The sun shining through behind it lit Tripplett's hair up like kindling. He had a thick moustache and horn-rimmed glasses, the look of a sax player, and an army jacket with his name over the right breast. He was driving a beat up silver Buick.

Tripplett looked like a power forward. He also looked like he hadn't had a really pleasant evening since about 1962. On the registration card, he listed Dothan, Alabama, as home.

"Can I get a drink anywhere?"

"The Harbor Side up there," I pointed behind Tripplett, "serves beer and wine."

"I'm talking about vodka and black pepper, not beer and wine."

I would have felt better if I were sure that the small movement of Tripplett's mouth was a smile rather than a nervous tic.

"Only place for hard stuff is The Parenthetical, in town." I left out Henri's, since I couldn't see Lou and Hank serving Tripplett the stuff he wanted in quantity.

I don't often send guests to The Parenthetical. Simon Charles runs the place, a tavern behind the insurance office, and Si doesn't like the company of travelers very much. In addition, although Tripplett seemed all right—and a Vet like Si was—there aren't many blacks in the area. Indians are the chief minority, as the natives say, and Si doesn't like their company either.

"What kind of name is that, Parenthetical?"

"Owner has a weakness for poetry."

Tripplett counted five fingers and said, "the word's got too many syllables to be poetry, man. Poems don't use five syllable words." When I couldn't answer, Tripplett added, "where's it at?"

I gave him directions and suggested that he mention Pilgrim's Harbor. That way Si would know I'd sent him and maybe go easy on the nigger jokes. Maybe. Tripplett looked as if slam-dunking would be effortless. I might have to deal with Si later.

"Serve in Vietnam?" I asked, since Tripplett didn't seem ready to leave.

"Never should have come back, neither."

It didn't take much to convey his feelings in the matter. I heard helicopters and machine guns, saw the challenge in Tripplett's glare, and decided not to ask the man's opinion about Presidential politics.

I hoped he wouldn't come back from The Parenthetical later in the evening ornery. Delbert Simmons couldn't get here fast enough to make a difference. If he could, it looked as if Tripplett would solve Delbert's suspenders problems by biting off his gut. The man was in playing shape.

***

After Tripplett left, I noticed that my Pinto was gone. I'd been hoping to catch a glimpse of Cindy when she got it.

Her bicycle, a ten-speed Nishiki Ultra Tour which the warden-turned-farmer father must have hocked his herd for, was leaning against the post that supported the big neon sign.

It was a state of the art, man's machine in gloss red and it looked ready to deal with the Rockies. Balanced against the post, her bike seemed to have its hands in its back pockets and be contemplating me as I registered my guests.

A man came in from a town called Defiance. He wore a little engineer's cap and the oldest jeans I'd ever seen. Looked like they'd been patched everywhere a person might bend and been washed ten thousand times.

"Wait, let me guess," I said. "Defiance, Maryland?"

The man shook his head, smiling. Train engineers love talk of towns.

"Not even close."

"Wisconsin? Nevada?"

"Negative." He leaned back against the door and rested his elbow on top of the stamp machine. I'd guessed his mood correctly.

"You're not a Yankee, are you? Defiance, Maine, doesn't look to be right."

"Defiance, Ohio. Yankee stock, though. Vermont. So you're right there."

"Alaska was my next guess."

"On the banks of the beautiful Maumee, an hour from Toledo and halfway to Fort Wayne. They always use the Maumee in crossword puzzles."

His name was Rex McCarter. His business, of course, was trains.

"They say it's a dying industry," I said.

"Not my kind of trains ain't."

"Then you must have cracked the European market."

McCarter frowned. Apparently, he could be teased about Defiance, but not about trains.

"I'm in miniature steam trains. Perfect scaled-down replicas of the 1830 locomotives, all the right details. I put it all together myself, the rails, the crossties, switches, the whole layout. Two or three cars, cute caboose. Anaheim to Bangor, I'll go anywhere to get a new minny established."

"And there's a demand?"

"You kidding?"

McCarter took off his hat and used it to wipe his entire face, pate to chin and all around the neck, slowly. It seemed an old ritual of patience, like what he'd do waiting for passengers to get on and off.

He was the sort of guest who required careful management. Easily offended on the topic of his business, he was nevertheless always talking about it, testing reactions.

"I figure amusement parks might have them, but they wouldn't work with a small operation, one guy, would they?"

"Rex McCarter wouldn't touch amusement parks, mister. I work with the communities. Hell, I'm everywhere. 'Lil Toot' and 'Old Toot' and 'Tom Thumb.' Put them through parks and a few acres of woods. The market's great."

"This is a new one on me," I said, raising a pen and registration card. McCarter didn't approach the counter.

"You mustn't get so out of touch." He frowned. I thought he was going to leave rather than check in to a place run by such a fool. "I tell you, I've got a waiting list would keep me going till I'm 96. Warm weather, kids ride all day. You find a guy can make a good buck just on weekends and summer."

With that, McCarter decided to stay. He chugged over and took the pen with a little cough.

"You do it all yourself?"

"Not any more. I package it. Best part is looking a site over, figuring out the arrangement. Just standing there seeing how it should go in and out of trees, over brooks on a bridge, out by the road. I'm Rex, the King, always the first to drive a new train and blow its whistle for real."

As he left for his room, McCarter swayed when he walked and moved at a continuously accelerating pace. It seemed like he was pulling out of a station. Tomorrow, when the Pumph cleans McCarter's room, she'll probably find cinders in the bed.

***

I didn't see Cindy return the Pinto either. No matter how anxious I was to catch sight of her, she managed to come and go without notice.

File that one away, Howser. The woman can do stealth.

It was 9:00 when I noticed the car was back and the bike gone. She hadn't stopped in to say hello, hadn't tapped on the window, hadn't waved. I liked to think she watched me deal with a couple of guests, stood outside beneath the fir seeing in although I couldn't see out. I liked to think she didn't want to bother me, didn't want to put me in an awkward position.

But I knew that, more likely, she was so engrossed in her plants that she didn't have a thought about me. I felt I was getting to know her.

I wondered what Cindy would have made of Selma Schultz from New Jersey. Mrs. Schultz checked in about 8:00 and at first I thought she was wearing some kind of costume. I was glad I caught the smile and held the comment, because it got clear quickly that Mrs. Schultz was neither in costume nor a good mood.

She couldn't have been five feet tall, with a great pile of stiffened hair somewhere between gold and rust. She wore a black suit with dark stockings and pumps. A double loop of pearls rested on her vast bosom.

Mrs. Schultz had the most enormous lips I've ever seen. They reminded me of the old wax-candy lips children wore at Halloween.

"I do not think I can stand it," she gasped as soon as the bell on the door quieted. She'd flung open the door, giving the bell a ferocious series of shakes.

"Can I help you?"

"Yes you can help me." She looked at me as if I were the one to be singled out in a lineup. "You can direct me to a real motel. I told my husband I'm not staying in a flea bag. He doesn't have enough nerve to come in and ask, so I did. Had to get out and come all the way in here from the car."

"I'm sorry."

"You have to tell me, you know. It's only ethical."

"What do you mean by a real motel?" Because of her novelty, I was too amused to be offended by Mrs. Schultz. Yet.

"You know perfectly well what I mean, young man. Don't be rude." She patted her hair, which shifted a few degrees left and stayed there. "A Holiday Inn, or at least a Best Western. I'm sure you haven't a Hilton in the entire state."

"There's a Holiday Inn 30 miles up."

The noise she made stopped just short of a scream. She put her hand to her chest.

"I knew it. We should never have come this way, I told Randolph that fifty times." She squinted at me. "You're not lying to me, are you? I'll turn you in if you are."

"I'm sorry, again. Things are widely spaced out here. Mostly, you find places like this one."

"A Ramada, maybe?"

"Not until tomorrow. And that's if you drive all day."

"Then I guess we're stuck, aren't we?" Mrs. Schultz said within an enormous exhale. I smelled something I hadn't smelled in years, recognizing instantly the bitter scent of Sen Sen.

"I'm sure you'll be comfortable here."

"Randolph will pay for this, mark my words. I'm not going to let him forget he made me stay at a place like this. Oh, no."

She opened the door viciously and barked something at the car. Then she jerked her thumb over her shoulder at me like an umpire calling a runner out.

When Randolph came in, she plopped down in a chair. Randolph didn't look at her, or at me.

"Please," he said, "give me your nicest room." The

way he said it, almost as a plea, was touching. I gave Randolph #15. Too bad he had to share it with Selma.

"You're not getting me to eat over there," she said while her husband filled out the card. She pointed to Harbor Side. "I'm drawing the line. Ptomaine I do not need."

"The only other restaurants are in town or at the mall," I said. "You might like Henri's, or maybe The No-Name Restaurant off Laurel Street."

"The No-Name Restaurant?" she asked. "Very imaginative. It's a good thing I have fruit in the car."

It amazed me that she had a man like Randolph for a mate. He was a good seventy-five and looked capable of walking across the Gobi. He'd traded in his hiking boots for a pair of tasseled loafers, but I assumed that was Selma's doing. His fingers, long and tapered, seemed suited only for the gentlest of stroking. The class of his dress and physique was undercut by a carriage that had shifted from erect to cringing. Enough strength remained to suggest, along with a slightly baffled expression, that he hadn't been under his wife's influence that long. I guessed it was a second marriage for each, with Randolph flabbergasted at his error in judgment.

Shortly after Randolph and Selma checked in, Buck Ticey made it a night for loudmouths. He was a sidewheeler, one of those men who talks out of the side of his mouth, too loud, as if he's at home only in the tavern.

"If your name was Thurston, you'd call yourself Buck too," he said when he'd put his American Express card back in his wallet.

"Thurston Ticey sounds impressive to me," I said. It wasn't good business to agree that a guest's name was strange.

"The third, I might add. Thurston Marcus Ticey III."

"Nice."

"I come from money."

Two in a row. If I didn't already feel sorry enough for Randolph Schultz, I'd be tempted to put Buck Ticey in the room next to Selma. It would be fun to listen while the two of them conversed.

Ticey was prowling around the office, touching things. He spun the rack where I keep postcards and brochures, pressed the button on the cigarette machine for matches, and flicked the Venetian blinds.

"Where are the women?" Ticey asked.

"Pardon?" I thought he might be talking to the gnome, which he was staring at and rubbing.

"Women. Where are the women around here?"

"The rooms are all done. They go home by 3:00, usually."

"I don't mean the maids, pal."

"Guess I don't know what you mean." The pimp trade isn't exactly lucrative around these parts any more.

"I've had nothing but losers ever since I crossed the Mississippi, you know what I mean? It's downright depressing. Can't you help me out?"

I shook my head.

"A phone number? A singles bar? Outcall service?"

"I can't be much help, Mr. Ticey."

"You sure looked like a nice enough guy."

"Maybe there's an R-rated movie over at the mall."

"Everyplace has to have a pussy shop. A hedge against the economy. I can make it worth your while, if that's what it takes."

I turned to the board where I keep the keys, trying to look busy. On the shelf below was a stack of papers. I began to sort them into meaningless piles. Ticey cleared his throat.

"Sir?" I looked back as if surprised to see him still there.

"You don't know what a bad string I've had." He began to pace again. "Last night was the worst. A coyote zero, that's what she was. You know what a coyote zero is?"

I didn't, but Ticey wasn't waiting to hear from me. He was rolling. I wished he'd put down the gnome.

"A coyote zero is when you're out late drinking in some bar till closing and the light's bad so you can't see the girl you take back to your motel, you're too loaded to notice anyway, you wake up the next morning and she's lying asleep on your arm, it's killing you, but you get a good look at her and instead of waking her so you can get up, you bite off your arm. That's a coyote zero. I was with one last night."

Ticey looked at me, a huge smile finally straightening his mouth. Satisfied, he headed for the door.

"Big Buck usually deals with tens," he said. "An occasional eight or nine, if the night's real bad."

I knew Ticey was trying to be friendly. But after Selma Schultz, I may have been edgy. Besides, I'd had complaints about the toilet in #8, hot water in #42, tv in #49, and the smell in #55. And I hadn't seen Cindy Bonds.

"It gets better after the Cascades," I said to Ticey. As he left, his car screeched out of the parking lot.

***

Just before midnight, when I was getting ready to leave, Tripplett came in with his army jacket slung over his shoulder.

Vodka and black peppers hadn't improved his mood.

He glared. I wondered if Simon Charles and the boys had given Tripplett a hard time at The Parenthetical. When he didn't speak for nearly a minute, I began to get nervous.

"Anything wrong, Mr. Tripplett?" At least my voice didn't crack.

"Never seen anything like it," he said. "Not in Nam, not down south, nowhere."

"Simon doesn't get many outsiders at The Parenthetical. I should have warned you."

"Talking about, man?"

"Just that I'm sorry I sent you there."

"Place was fine. Nobody gives me trouble if we've had combat in common. Si's good."

I was relieved to hear that. Tripplett wasn't going to flatten me. But he did continue to glare.

"So what happened?"

I saw a pickup turn in. It would be Mike Strummer, the kid who watches Pilgrim's Harbor until late morning. He was new in the business, but responsible. The Pruitts assigned him to the night shift and odd jobs the first year.

"This guy you got staying here," Tripplett said. "Buck something. I thought you said you don't send your guests to that bar."

"I don't. He must have found it by chance, looking for a ten."

"The man can ruin a nice night. He works hard for tail, though, I've got to give him that much. Loud and lewd and pure jive. Even this old gal your friend Simon keeps around the bar wouldn't leave with Big Buck. I've never seen anything like it."

Mike Strummer opened the door behind Tripplett, who spun around in a crouch and pointed his knuckles at the intruder. Strummer held his hands up, palms open and facing Tripplett. No weapons, see? He edged around the big man and smiled. The kid had a wide smile that creased everything up and buried his nose in his upper lip. Tripplett relaxed.

"Go on home, Dewey. Sorry I'm late."

"No problem. This is Mr. Tripplett. Room 37."

"I know," Strummer said. "Si already told me about the guy's skill with Stoly. That's why I'm late."

Still muttering about Buck Ticey, Tripplett left with a grunt. But Strummer's comment had helped.

"Didn't know you stopped in for a drink before work," I said.

"I don't. Si makes the best cheesesteak sandwiches outside of Philadelphia," Strummer answered.

I went through the register with Strummer and got him ready for his shift. By the time I left, all I wanted was some wine and a good, hard sleep.

CHAPTER SIXTEEN

For a June 29th, the night was cool. A sweater would have been nice, or something to help with the north wind.

Hazy nights here often feel clear, so that when I looked up and didn't see stars it was a surprise. The sounds were right for clear, the smell was crisp enough, and there was an oddly pure light, but it was clouded over.

I thought it might be the absence of humidity. The area was a meteorologist's nightmare, today's puzzle with tomorrow's clues.

Cindy had put my keys back behind the visor. Her clove smell was still in the car.

I closed my eyes and rested against the head support. My arm fell limp on the seat and smacked against a clay pot.

She had left a Swedish ivy for me on the passenger seat, with a note. "Just a little water and only low light. It should thrive. I'll show you how to prune it (you don't seem like a plant person). Thank you for the favor. I'll call soon. Cindy."

I drove home slowly, hand on the pot so it wouldn't tip when I turned. I was glad no one was around to see me lug the plant upstairs.

I cleared a place for it on the credenza, which I shoved down closer to the window. Cradling a mug of Hearty Burgundy in my palms, I sat in front of the ivy drowsing, imagining myself doing something else with my life.

What would it have been like if I were a butcher, an architect, a podiatrist, a shortstop, or a haberdasher? In high school in Milwaukee, I couldn't concentrate when we had the mandatory sessions with guidance counselors to discuss career options. I'd get lost in fantasies about the occupations they'd propose, seeing myself in a suit talking to a jury, in uniform flying a jet, in a hard-hat welding beams. I thought I would try trucking, physical therapy. I imagined myself on a tv soap opera.

But all I knew how to do was move around. I knew how to make do in a new town fast, how to find what I needed. At least, I would tell himself, I do know what I need.

Late at night, I sometimes like to sit with a mug of wine and flash through the options. It helps reduce my occasional restlessness, especially when I'm too tired to carve.

Suddenly, the room began to fill with wood chips. Stacks of *The Courier* levitated on beds of pine shavings that were so thin I couldn't see them. A strong wind was taking over every corner of the room.

There was a huge chunk of wood where the hide-a-bed should be and a figure detached itself from within the chunk, sat up and stared at me. Golden haired and green eyed.

A noise came from behind the place where the chips came flying into the room. It was footsteps.

No, it was the sound of a knife against wood. It was the sound of a hand smoothing and smoothing wood, a hand giving its oils over into the wood.

I was having trouble breathing. I was covered with wood chips.

Their taste was in my mouth. Their texture was a track I could follow from nose to lungs.

My hands moved as if swimming up for air. I began to shape the chips into the form of a woman, which grew hard and smooth with my touch.

I awoke with a start. Burgundy sloshed over the mug's rim onto my wrist.

I looked to the window where the Swedish ivy was at peace. Squat in its pot, very lush and dark green, it seemed ready to start bringing order to the place.

That, of course, was it. The feeling of depression and restlessness lifted and I got my second wind.

I finished the wine and arranged myself within the mound on the hide-a-bed. Tomorrow I'll begin to clean up. I'll make the plant feel at home.

CHAPTER SEVENTEEN

I slumped on the hide-a-bed trying to reimagine my living room space. It was sunny outside, but the morning was cooler than last night had been.

Bags are the answer. Thirty gallon, dark green trash bags. Lord bless polyethylene plastic.

I was sure I could get all the soiled clothes in one bag. I could get the carving paraphernalia in another, old magazines and papers in a third. Buy three-ply.

Another bag could probably hold all the kitchen clutter. Lugging them down to the alley could be a trick, but if the bags hold and my shoulder stays in joint, the program should work.

It's simple, like any good engineering solution. There was a time in Chicago when I considered a career in engineering. Until I saw the prerequisites. While I wasn't sure what I could do, I knew what I couldn't. Geometry and algebra were out.

The trash bag plan occurred to me as I lay awake this morning looking at the Swedish ivy. Its thick, scalloped-edged leaves packed tightly together in the pot suggested stability, a missing element in my environment.

Once I get everything bagged, I can build shelves, buy a hamper and a parson's table or two at Westview Center. Then I'll de-bag and everything will have a place. It'll be like repotting the Swedish ivy.

I tried to imagine shelves in the apartment. They wouldn't be a rickety, build-it-yourself set of gray metal decks that swayed whenever you took down a book, either. They would be held firm with toggle bolts. I'd have a wicker hamper with handles, and parson's tables with heft. Nothing in purple plastic.

I'll have breakfast at home more often as well. A little discipline. The working kitchen is a neat kitchen, etcetera.

For instance, how about a food processor? Not a Cuisinart, perhaps, but something consistent with a Pinto and Pilgrim's Harbor: something with a couple of slicing disks and a guard to keep me from cutting my hand off, a blade for dough so I can make Cindy whole wheat loaves.

***

It became a morning of rain blown sideways by the wind, the kind of rain that is heavy and cold, that demands you think about November sleet. It hit the window as hard as hail, blurred the MOBIL sign and the roof of Pilgrim's Harbor.

I stripped the sheets and folded up the hide-a-bed, which groaned at the unaccustomed exertion. Dust covered the carpet underneath like dew. The February issue of *Chip Chats*, splotched with wine, turned up along with my plastic hair brush, brown socks, an empty pizza carton from Giacomo's of Westview, and an array of glasses and utensils.

I wrapped myself in a blanket against the cold. In four trips, I moved everything into the kitchen that belonged there. I moved each piece of furniture to a new location, shook out the rug, and ran a dustcloth over anything hard. Patience and logic would be the keys.

***

After a Yuban and two slices of white bread, I went out to purchase bags. As part of my new program, I bought Raisin Bran, bananas, and skim milk. The last time I ate Raisin Bran was when my mother told me I ate faster than our dog. I'd only been trying to finish them before they got soggy. Remembering the stacks of magazines, I bought a ready-to-assemble rack for the living room and an extra set of braces to make it taut.

By 11:00, when I could see floors and countertops, the telephone rang. It was Mike Strummer at Pilgrim's Harbor, in a panic.

I quieted him, trying to make sense of his ramblings. Mike never called for help before.

Since the apartment already looked better than it had in months, I hurried in to help him. It would be good to have something more to accomplish tomorrow morning.

I got to Pilgrim's Harbor within five minutes, expecting to find Delbert Simmons on the premises adjusting his Mariners cap and working his suspenders. A fire truck or ambulance, perhaps. But the front of the office was barren and things seemed still.

Inside, the air was thick with scent of lilac. Mike, Selma Schultz, and Randolph Schultz stood frozen, like they were in a publicity photograph for a play. Besides Selma's perfume, all I could sense was everyone's full-fledged rage.

Mrs. Schultz wouldn't pay her bill. Last night, in all the confusion, I'd neglected to make her pay in advance.

Randolph sat on a stool as if still outside, balanced against the car fender. His handsome head was in his hands. He seemed to have lost weight overnight, although I didn't get a good look at him last night in all the commotion. Maybe Selma ate all the fruit.

"There he is!" she roared when I came in. Her lips had spread and were now nearly nose-to-chin and cheek-to-cheek.

"Mrs. Schultz, good morning."

"I told this child that I would simply not deal with an underling. It's bad enough I have to deal with you."

"Didn't you sleep well?"

She looked as if she always slept well, as if sleep would not have the nerve to fail her. I was trying to find a useful approach, like a pilot in a storm.

"Don't think for one moment that I intend to pay

your outrageous price. For a cubbyhole like that you should get $10 and not a penny more."

She had me. I can't imagine why I didn't collect last night.

"I'm sorry you weren't happy with the room. You should have asked to be moved."

"Don't tell me what I should have done! Besides, I'm quite certain it wouldn't have made any difference, unless you were prepared to move me to a Hilton."

"Would you like to fill out a complaint form?"

I motioned to Strummer, who went into the little room behind the office. But Mrs. Schultz simply guffawed.

"There isn't enough time," she seemed to say. She also seemed to be laughing.

She flicked open her purse and withdrew a ten, placed it on the counter, and jerked her hand back as if my touching the bill at the same time she did might contaminate her. From the way she had the ten handy, I was certain this was part of a practiced scam. She turned to leave.

"I'm afraid this won't do," I said. "Your bill isn't settled."

"So call my lawyer, F. Lee Bailey."

She yanked open the door, sending the bell into another paroxysm, and rushed outside. Randolph followed, off-balance, as if having been sucked out by the force of her leaving. I was astonished to see how quickly she could move.

"Just a moment..."

"Get me out of here this instant, Randolph. Don't you ever do this to me again."

Randolph somehow reached their car first. He held the door open for her and Selma slid in, pulling it out of his grip and sending him teetering. He fell against the door as it shut, narrowly missing a set of crushed fingers.

Sprinting around to the driver's side, starting the car before he shut his door, screeching out of the lot, Randolph moved as if well-practiced. OK, so they knew what they were doing all along. I hoped the sixteen bucks they saved made the Schultzes happy.

Mike Strummer peeped in. He didn't know whether to laugh or call Delbert Simmons.

"What are we going to do," I asked, "issue an all-points bulletin for Selma Schultz, the infamous lady in lips?"

"I'm sorry I had to call, Dewey. Why don't I come in an hour early tonight and make it up to you?"

"Forget it." But while I had Strummer in this mood, I decided to spring the Fourth on him. "What you can do is give me an extra hand for the holiday. I've got an idea for a party and we're going to be short of maids."

Strummer's eyes registered only slight distress, then he smiled and shrugged. A smart kid. It would be a good experience for him, just what he needs at this stage of his career.

Career. I had to laugh, thinking that I wasn't being much of a mentor if I couldn't face down the likes of Selma Schultz. I remembered when I used to think of my job as a stage in my career. Onwards and upwards. But moving up would mean moving out, away, and I was never quite ready to do that again.

"What kind of party?" Strummer asked.

"Something I've been meaning to try for years. A little gaiety for the guests on Independence Day."

"You talking hats and noisemakers, a flag in every room?"

"Well, I was thinking of a cookout and punch by the pool. Dogs and corn, maybe, at 10:00."

"Real punch?" He perked up.

"I think so. We'll get some cherry Hi-C and lace it with vodka. Color some ice cubes blue. Float some marshmallows on top. Can't you just see it? Looks like the flag and it'll be real heart-warming for the guests."

"Who pays?"

"I'm working on that. Mr. Pruitt's a history buff."

"And a tightwad."

"I'll approach him with the good advertising slant."

"What happens if you get another guest like Mrs. Schultz that night?"

"I've been in this business a long time, Mike. There isn't another guest like Mrs. Schultz."

I walked back to my little room and sat on the recliner. Strummer followed.

"I hope you're right," he said. "At least she came early in my career."

"There isn't another Thurston Marcus Ticey III either. Every guest is unique, if you take the time to see it. You'll find this a useful principle in life as well."

"I see what you mean."

"Did you catch Ticey's act?"

"Catch it? He asked me for Alla Mae's phone number."

I nodded and cranked back. The water stain shone out of the ceiling like a dulled sun.

"You just have to hope for a good mix," I said. "One night to the next."

"With fifty nine units, the odds on a good mix aren't all that favorable."

"We're not social directors. We don't wear whistles around our necks."

"Then why the party? Fourth of July, the place will fill up without it."

Strummer was in his early twenties. He was a tall kid with freckles, big hands, and an elongated chest. I looked up at him and smiled, suddenly feeling very old and full of mature affection.

"Because the guests want company on the Fourth. It's the only night that ever happens, but I see it every year. It takes care of itself."

***

Three years ago, there had been an impromptu softball game in the street out front. In return for the home plate umpiring assignment, I was able to persuade Delbert Simmons to put up the Department's only two barricades at one end of the street and park his car at the other.

Guests divided themselves neatly into two teams, east vs. west. After a quick poll of home states, they decided to use the Mississippi River as the dividing line.

The Gaylord Frombachs from Brampton, Ontario, didn't play but took two rolls of film. They sent them to me the following fall and the pictures are still on the office wall by the brochures.

The year before that was music. It seemed that a dozen guests had teenaged children with them, each with a portable stereo radio and tape deck. At first, the cacophony threatened to disrupt everything.

But I was able to convince most of the kids not to play their tapes. Instead, I called Handsome Harry Hambleton, the local disk jockey at KUTE-AM, and got him to play the top fifty songs of the year. Then the kids all turned their machines to 1175 on the dial and blasted the songs into the pool area. There was dancing, even among parents, and the Peter Barleys from Utica, New York, brought out a case of American whiskey.

On my first Fourth of July here, we had a preponderance of senior citizens for some reason. These things, I've come to understand, cannot always be explained. Why 68% of the guests one night should be over 70, or 80% from New England, or half wearing blue, I would not presume to guess. That year, it was seniors.

There were spontaneous card games all along the walkway from the office to the rooms. People dragged tables and folding chairs out of their cars and set them up in the shade. Pinochle, gin rummy, poker, casino. There didn't seem to be much in the way of gambling, but excitement filled the air.

Many of the women went on walks around the perimeter of Pilgrim's Harbor. Arm in arm, women from Lansing, Michigan, were strolling with women from Orange, Texas, as if on a promenade. Two women who had grown up in Muskingum County, Ohio, during the 1920s found themselves in adjacent rooms. They walked together comparing acquaintances, although they'd never heard of one another before. A white-haired woman from Salina, Kansas, stood back to back with an approximately red-haired woman from Parsippany, New Jersey, measuring to determine which woman was taller.

I'd never before considered interfering with the Fourth of July process. But the idea of providing a little refreshment and courtesy was appealing. Nothing that would keep them up too late, nothing to make their departure in the morning less timely, just some simple hospitality on a bit larger scale than normal.

CHAPTER EIGHTEEN

"Is this Mr. Dewey Howser?" the voice asked.

"Speaking."

"Mr. Howser, I'm Jason Ladue. Jay Ladue. Professor Finfer told me to give you a call."

"Oh yes, I've been expecting to hear from you. You'll be coming through here, then."

"I figure on July 2nd. Unless my car lets me down."

"When Mr. Finfer, I mean Professor Finfer, didn't call I thought maybe he couldn't get hold of you."

"Haven't you heard? Oh, probably not, it's not exactly national news. The guy that was running against our candidate in the primary dropped out. His wife was having an affair with some contractor, some big contributor to the campaign. I guess the professor's too busy to call at this point."

"Sounds juicy. I'll keep a room available. It doesn't matter what time you get here."

"He told me to ask you a favor, by the way. He wondered if you'd be extra sure not to let his briefcase out of your sight. I think that the contractor gave big to our campaign too. Only you've got the proof."

***

Alla Mae agreed to help decorate for the Fourth. Her expression told me she thought the idea was absurd, but it wasn't something she'd refuse to do.

There's a busboy at Harbor Side, an industrious high school junior named Gilliam who's looking for ways to earn extra cash. I might be able to get him to help, too. And I've got Mike Strummer.

I'll need the help, especially now with news of a big

family coming to stay for the holiday. I'm already losing my enthusiasm for this party, now that I know there's an invasion planned.

I've got a precedent for concern. Alla Mae was at Pilgrim's Harbor that time in 1978, when another big family came through and nearly destroyed their room. I was still new on the job.

It was a family from northern Oklahoma. The father kept saying, as if he'd memorized it phonetically, that they were from outside Ponca City. From outside Ponca City, nearby the Arkansas River.

They had nine kids, all ages, and a couple of grandparents. I think I remember that the oldest kid was an aunt. Thirteen people in all, and they took two rooms.

I was too intimidated to see if it violated any codes. They were a mean looking crew. I just collected the money and turned over the keys.

The next morning, Alla Mae had walked right into it. By the time I got there, she had calmed but the vinegar smell was overwhelming.

Apparently, the Ponca City clan had filled up balloons with a mixture of vinegar, shampoo, alcohol, sugar, and honey. Some other substances too. Delbert Simmons stood in the middle of it later writing things like *ordure, urine, brylcreem* in his note pad.

They had filled all the glasses in both rooms with the vinegar mixture, then propped them on door ledges and where they would be sure to get kicked over. Dumped a potful on the carpets for good measure.

The goo was everywhere. Walls, beds, toilets, windows, drapes. They had even stuffed some in the locks. Alla Mae kept talking about the chocolate and peanut butter, about ants going to inhabit her hair. Seeing her that upset was a shock for everyone who knew her.

Now another big family is coming to Pilgrim's Harbor. It gets me where I'm most vulnerable and makes me flash back to that earlier experience. I don't trust groups of kin that travel in packs and squeeze into rooms too small to hold them.

I took the call for advance reservations this evening. They'll be staying July 3 through July 6. Three nights of it.

Pilgrim's Harbor doesn't get many advance reservations. Occasionally, a guest plans his stops a day ahead and calls. Or there's a planamaniac, who has to know six months in advance where he's staying each night of the trip. Now here's two in one day—Jay Ladue and then the Hazelriggs. It's not normal.

Jerome and Rachel Hazelrigg. Topeka, Kansas. One room, two double beds. Their sons, Clarence and Alvin. One room, two double beds. Their daughters, Naomi, Janet, Paula, and Monica. One room, two double beds.

I hadn't asked for their names. Hazelrigg just gave them to me, spelling each slowly and saying it didn't matter if the rooms were close to each other. Any arrangements would do.

I confirmed their reservations and quoted Hazelrigg $271.50 for three nights, plus tax. The two extra girls in the third room explained the additional cost.

Hazelrigg hadn't seemed concerned. I don't know why this worries me.

Anybody traveling with six and popping for that kind of nightly sleep probably *would* call ahead. He must want to be off the road when everybody else was driving. That makes sense. Avoid becoming another holiday statistic. But Pilgrim's Harbor wasn't exactly a Marriott in Nashville. Why here?

Because it's along the way, I told myself. Because

it's where the compass passed through when Hazelrigg worked out the radius of his summer trip.

Maybe it's Kansas. I associate Kansas with dryness, right or wrong. Bad, violent weather; heat. Buffalo grass with parched skulls, wheatfields and Dodge City.

How could it be Kansas? Topeka is no Wichita but it has its almost 120,000. Has the largest psychiatric center in the country, the Menninger Foundations, and all those hospitals. Maybe that has something to do with it. That, and Hazelrigg's dry, crackling voice, his parched gasp, and the wonder of why anyone in his right mind would pick Pilgrim's Harbor for a Fourth of July three-nighter.

To offset my jitters, I decided to talk Cindy into coming to the party. I'll see to it that there's a plate of vegetables with yogurt dip.

***

Dolfy Toskol has it all arranged. It's amazing what the guy got accomplished with us suspicious natives.

We're going to use Pilgrim's Harbor as the start and finish points. Jock Pruitt loved the idea (Toskol is an expert on eighteenth century American history, which is the subject of his September lecture at Stanford). The race will be called the Pilgrim's Harbor Fourth of July Fun Run and in return for the publicity Pruitt is donating the parking lot.

Delbert Simmons has agreed to help out. Toskol somehow got to Alla Mae, turned on the charm, and convinced her to help at the finish line. Half the staff will join her.

Toskol got flyers printed up for free by Lou Pumphrey's old semi-pro teammate, Wilbur "Creampuff" Hambleton, who is the dj's father and a famous spitball pitcher. The flyers are bright red, with enormous black letters. To enter, people just tear off the bottom of the flyer and bring it to Room #41 of Pilgrim's Harbor.

"I've only got four entries so far," Toskol told me. "But pre-registration's always slow, even for a big race."

"Who sent in so far?"

"Let's see. I'm keeping a list here somewhere." He rummaged around in his pocket. "A kid named Gilliam that works up at Harbor Side, used to run in high school. I'm a little worried about him beating me, but he seems out of shape. There's a guy who works out at the mall, in a sporting goods store. That would be Mel Salvo. There's me. And there's a woman from the college named Bonds. Keep the faith, brother, and we'll have a splendid race."

***

A couple came in, stopped by the door, and began kissing. It was a very serious kiss, eyes closed, hands roaming up and down each other's backs, legs on the move. I looked away, but had no trouble hearing the couple breathe and lick.

When they were done, they looked at each other without speaking and kept at that twice as long as they'd kissed. They joined hands and drifted to the counter.

"A room," he said.

"For the night," she said.

I wondered if Scott Conner and his wife Pamela had been doing this all the way from Silver Springs, Maryland, which they listed as home.

"Two doubles or a queen?" I asked, unable to resist. Demure Pamela Conner glanced aside.

"The queen will be acceptable," Conner said.

I could see in his face, despite the exercise Mrs. Conner was giving it, the look of preliminary judgments and conference calls, the look of the law. No one talked like young Washington lawyers, no one moved across an office like them, no one held the spouse's hand like them. Spines stiff as bound volumes of law, edges thumbed, elbows crooked. Conner had on a striped tie, loose at the collar, and the long sleeves of his pink Oxford shirt were rolled up three tucks.

"Is it appropriate to ask," Conner inquired, "whether I can or cannot use the pool of an evening?"

"Open till ten."

"Would it be possible, in that case, to do two things? One: to purchase swim suits, since we seem to have misplaced both mine and Mrs. Conner's. And two: to have cocktails sent to our room?"

They stood with arms around each other's waists. When he finished his speech, Conner looked to his wife and smiled. She nodded approval. His lips moved as though he were counting how long each gesture should last.

"Cocktails are a problem. The Harbor Side only serves beer and wine. I don't know if you can get them to go."

"Beer is a beverage neither I nor Mrs. Conner would consume. Wine, while certainly potable, is not what we had envisioned at this time. The wine we shall drink is wine we have brought with us for that purpose."

"And the trunks?" Mrs. Conner asked.

"The suits. Swim suits, actually."

"Sorry again," I said. "Nearest place would be in Westview Center Mall, back past the Interstate."

"Oh, dear," she said.

"I'm afraid my wife has a certain affliction, a phobia, if you will, of the type of environment typified by the standard shopping center or mall. I shall have to go there alone. Now the question becomes: do I wish to leave Pamela for the time it would take to purchase swim suits at this mall?"

"Or the corollary, dear: do you wish to purchase these swim suits badly enough to leave me for the time it would take to do so?"

Conner turned to his wife. He patted her shoulder and smiled. "I appreciate your input."

They kissed again.

"It shouldn't take more than fifteen minutes," I said after a polite half-minute. No response. "That's total time, Pilgrim's Harbor to Westview Center, buy the suits, drive back."

"Yes," Conner said. "But this is our vacation, you understand."

"He is gone frequently because of his job. Scotty is an attorney at law." She looked up at him although they were about the same size. "He also specializes in the preparation of expert witnesses before trial. Therefore, he is gone frequently."

"There are many demands," Conner said.

"Well, like I said, you could probably pick up those swim suits inside of fifteen minutes."

"An establishment like yours perhaps should consider acquiring the sort of vending machine which dispenses items such as swim suits. It is possible that such an investment would prove cost-beneficial in a rather short space of time."

"Further," Mrs. Conner added, "additional items such as swim caps, nose plugs, perhaps some tanning lotions, shampoo, or razor blades could be offered. These would reduce payback time significantly."

"Pamela is of great help to me in my work."

I thanked them for their advice. Conner turned at the door, fully disentangling himself from his wife for the first time since they'd arrived. He pointed toward the ceiling with his pinky.

"Is there something else?" I asked. Conner had adequately trained me to respond as he wished.

"One must assume local ordinances constrain your ability to offer on the premises what is commonly called hard liquor. Perhaps it would be in the best interests of operators such as yourself to make it known that you would respond favorably to a consideration of such an ordinance."

"That," Mrs. Conner added, "is the democratic way."

"Like many women, and no doubt like many patrons of your establishment, Mrs. Conner does not enjoy bars," her husband said.

***

Cindy was finally reachable. She called just after 10:00 and sounded friendly.

"When do you usually wake up?" she asked.

"When the alarm goes off."

"Then why not set it for five?"

"That's, um, a little earlier than it usually goes off."

"But I like morning hikes."

"You mean we're going on a hike?"

"If you can get to the mall early enough to make it worth my while. I think that would be kind of nice to do on the first of July."

"Let's take one more shot at how early is early enough, so I can be sure I heard you right."

"What say six?"

"I suppose I could manage six. Keeping rigorous hours worked for monks. OK, I'll do it for the bulk."

"I'll bring Abelard."

"I trust that's the beagle?"

She chuckled. "It's the beagle."

"I thought you weren't going to name the dogs so it wouldn't hurt to give them away."

"Changed my mind. This one's very philosophical. Wrinkled brow, head cocked sideways, very inquisitive bark."

We agreed to walk the clear-cut. Cindy will bring a pack and we'll eat up there. I'll bring recommendations of other places for us to hike on future mornings. This was a favorable sign, I thought.

"I'm not in very good shape," I said. "I should probably warn you about that."

"We'll get you there by going slow. Remember that pace is everything."

"Say, I didn't know you were a runner. I heard you're going to be in that race we're sponsoring."

"You're sponsoring? Dolfy Toskol told me you wouldn't have anything to do with the race."

"That little squirt sure gets around." I shouldn't have given him such a nice room. "Wait a minute: he never asked me to help."

"If you wanted to, you should have volunteered. That's what the running scene is all about."

"Apropos of nothing, what time do you have to wake up to meet me at six? I mean, wouldn't it make more sense for me to come to your place and pick you up?"

"No. I won't go to sleep after work."

She didn't seem to be playing for the mystery. I couldn't imagine why she didn't want me to know where she lived. In time, I suppose.

"You'll get bags under your eyes."

"Haven't yet and I've kept these hours for years. One more thing: either get a bicycle or an asbestos suit. I don't like riding in Pintos."

***

Following her call, I had difficulty concentrating on my last guests of the night. On an ordinary night, several would have been excellent company. But I was clock-watching and formal. I even postponed making my list of things to do for the Fourth.

Sebastien Young took the 59th room and pulled me out of the distracted mood. A wild-looking Canadian, about 40, Young was so robust and ardent that I couldn't resist his spell.

"You people down here are so glum, so serious. What is it, the heat? Business bad?"

"Just tired. It's been a long day."

Young had his arms outstretched and was waving them in small circles. Twenty or thirty in one direction, then as many in reverse. He bent to touch the floor with his palms, knees stiff, twenty repetitions, talking all the while.

"I don't just mean you," he said. "Everybody I met this trip was bogged down. Don't understand it. This is the summertime, man, and people are trudging. How are they going to be come February? I mean, why travel if they do nothing but just plow ahead?"

He talked about a safari he'd been on last winter and the humorless computer manufacturer from Arlington who finally got his kill. Young managed to criticize for ten minutes, through a set of sit-ups and knee-bends, without seeming prejudiced.

"Maybe," I suggested, "we're all saving it for the big holiday?"

Young ignored me. "I was watching the cars all day," he said. Then he turned to lean against the door with his hands, feet planted a yard back, and began a series of vertical push-ups designed to stretch his achilles tendons. "Watched those cars and the only animation I detected was a mother turned around trying to smack her kid. Nobody was even talking. Reminded me of what some lady once wrote: A herd of elephants pacing along as if they had an appointment at the end of the world."

"I guess people don't travel by Interstate to take in the sights."

"Just going somewhere, huh?" Young searched through his suitcase and came out with a set of hand-grips. They were enormous black-handled things; I wasn't sure I could get my hand open far enough to grip one. I'd probably have to press it with both hands to get it moving. But Young squeezed them like they were rubber balls. "Couple days of that and I'd feel eaten up, a meal for maggots."

***

After Sebastien Young left with his key, I worked on the register and papers, waiting for Mike Strummer. I wasn't tired anymore.

Pilgrim's Harbor is close enough to the Interstate to let the night traffic be visible. I don't hear the noise anymore, unless I listen for it, but I enjoy watching all the vehicle lights—especially the rigs of semis—at the close of my business day.

I stepped out of the office. The evening was helped by the barely restrained, light wind which was as close to a calm breeze as we would get until September.

The trucks, as they cleared the overpass, seemed to dip their heads a moment before showing the pattern of their rear mounted lights. They dwarfed the few cars that passed, the night drivers trying to make up the miles.

I'm not sure I understood Sebastien Young's point, though what he said bothered me. People glumly going somewhere else all the time, impatient and irritable. I suppose it's a kind of lust. But I make my living off people like that, the en routers, so what did that make me?

It's a big country. How does a guy like Young expect people to get out and see Aunt Marge or the Grand Canyon?

You get on the big road, set the cruise control, and hold onto the wheel. Few people had the luxury of time to enjoy the getting there.

With NO turned on above the Pilgrim's Harbor VACANCY sign, my night was spent. I like it to happen late so there's a minimum of down-time.

Thinking of meeting Cindy at 6:00, I felt for the first time since our encounter five days ago that she was going to be a risk. Our appointment came quickly, as chance beginnings and ends both do, and she was unlike any woman I had been attracted to before. Measuring the space in my life, I wondered if I really had room for this woman.

All in all, I decided, it was perhaps time for a change. I didn't hear Mike Strummer come up behind me, but when he touched my shoulder, I didn't jump.

CHAPTER NINETEEN

July is a bad month for presidents. Seven of them died during July.

And the Fourth is particularly bad. Both John Adams and Thomas Jefferson went on the same Fourth, in 1826. Five years later, to the day, it was James Madison. On the other hand, Calvin Coolidge was born on the Fourth.

There were symbolic deaths, too. Warren Harding ate something he shouldn't have during a boat trip with his wife in July. He hung on till August 2. Richard Nixon was finished in July. The Supreme Court ruled against him and the House began to pass impeachment articles. Although it took him until August to quit, he was through in July. Andrew Johnson, the other impeachee, also died in July.

This is the sort of thing that makes me worry about what's coming along. Especially since things seem to be getting out of hand just as July begins. But I'm not ready to panic yet. After all, we first walked on the moon in July.

***

At 5:30 in the morning, I was the kind of tired that starts as a high. My blood was flowing thick and sweet as syrup, carrying its odd nourishment through the system and making everything from cuticle to follicle seem as bubbly as soda. I rolled down the car windows for crosswind. The morning air seemed enriched with nitrous oxide.

All the times I've been to Westview Center on my days off, I never really appreciated its spread before.

Seeing the empty parking lot at 6:00 made me realize how much land is involved.

A delivery truck could use a tank of gas just getting around back.

I turned left into the lot. It was like pulling onto the country estate in winter with all the trees bare on its demesne. Old Westview.

The mall looked more than closed. It looked abandoned.

I remembered the photo of Westview Center mounted inside, above the directory, showing it on the day it opened. Hot air balloons and a small parade, elk burgers by the west wing, a free Dodge Dart.

That aerial view never impressed me. It makes the mall look like a dried-up lake, shrunken and cracked. But this morning, coming into the parking lot, I saw the mall as monumental, something like a ruin restored.

Ignoring the crop of parking strips in orderly rows, I drove across the field of asphalt on the diagonal looking for Cindy against the building's gray face. At the east entrance, I saw her crouched beside the mailbox rearranging things inside her backpack. It was an extra-strength model, three feet high with a staunch frame, and looked like a chunk of steel disguised as royal blue nylon.

The pack seemed to have dozens of pouches. I hoped she wasn't planning on having me carry the cargo all day, unless the thing had wheels I couldn't see.

"Glad to see you're on time," she mumbled without looking up. I stayed in the car.

"Always ready to serve. The Innkeeper's Creed."

"I used to know a guy who said things like that. The tennis pro at the Walla Walla Country Club; thought he was clever." She shifted positions to get better leverage, one arm deep within the pack. "But he was a lightweight. Used to call me up for a date and the phone wouldn't even ring."

I tried to ignore what she said and how she said it. "I hope there's nothing breakable in there."

"Just trying to get the hard corners hidden." She shoved and something gave. "It's easier on the ribs."

"Tell me something. Why do you want to hike in a clear cut?"

I rested my chin on the windowframe. Cindy tied the flap and tested the pack for balance.

"Lots of people like to walk in graveyards," she said.

She wore a faded pair of old denim overalls and a plaid flannel workshirt that was mostly red. Her boots had a good eight hundred miles on them. At the collar, I could see the pale blue tee shirt she had worn the day we met.

"Not much left to see up there, you know. The Little Forest That Isn't. It's just a bunch of rubble."

"Are you going to get out and help, or is this just Critic's Corner?" She stood and looked at me, her eyes frosted. "You just have to know what to look for."

I yawned to ease the tension, opened the door, and slipped out. Once beside her, I stretched—a long and luxurious stretch like a lion in the zoo—and inhaled deeply.

I didn't like the idea of walking empty miles with Cindy sour. When I spoke to her last, she was all sweetness.

"Where's Abelard?" I made an elaborate show of looking around for the puppy. "Isn't he car trained yet?"

"Left him home. Didn't want you to feel threatened."

I detest this sort of tension, which explains my devotion to keeping guests calm. I got up at 5:30 for this?

It was time to try the Trusty Scout routine. Maybe

Cindy would be susceptible.

"Last time I was up there, the northwest quadrant of the clear cut was a regular shooting gallery—hubcaps, beercans, an old foot locker." She maintained her blank stare, but I let my momentum carry me. "Half a victrola, some orange juice jugs. So I thought maybe we should walk southeast from the ridge."

She nodded and handed me the backpack. There was no trace of warmth in her face.

I didn't know how she'd gotten to the mall or when. If she started from downtown, it was quite a walk. Maybe that explained her foul mood. I started to ask, but she stopped me after "How did . . . ?"

"Some friends told me about it," she answered a different question. "Back home, this one guy had a map with pins stuck in where the lumber companies did their heaviest cutting. Had a huge red cluster right here by your fair city."

"And you couldn't wait to see it?" I wondered if Cindy was about to use me for some kind of weird demonstration. I could visualize *The Courier*: Down with Lumbering, Local Innkeeper Protests.

"With my own two eyes," she said.

"You know, when I was in school, we had a Marx Brothers poster on our wall. *Duck Soup.*"

Her laugh was one she might use when an Irish Wolfhound pup tumbled over its enormous feet trying to race downhill. Silly thing.

She got in the car. I stashed the pack in the backseat and shut the door after her. Even that little gallantry drew a smirk.

The drive past Pilgrim's Harbor to Sullivan Reservoir was quiet, as it had been the other day. But it was charged in a different way and I was ready to acknowledge the July whammy.

I tried to think of topics we might have in common. Western life, travel, observing people. But I had the feeling that today she might turn on me even if I spoke up for saving the whales.

I glanced at her quickly, then back at the road. She seemed to be asleep.

***

Past the reservoir, the county road runs beside the river for three miles, narrowing as it turns away and then uphill steeply. It becomes a blacktop without markings, then a dirt lane darkened by overhanging trees.

This had been the main logging road during the peak years. It's crisscrossed by a half dozen other roads as if laid out by a stoned engineer. The side roads are overgrown now.

We reached the clear cut more quickly than I'd anticipated. As I slowed, the light that suddenly filled the treeless sky made it difficult to breathe.

"What's wrong?" Cindy was looking at me while I gaped. Her voice had almost become human again.

"I don't know. You could put thirty-five Westview Centers in here and not fill the space."

"Exactly." She rubbed her eyes like a child. "A forest fire without the fire. Welcome to Stump National Forest, boys and girls."

We got out and I shouldered the pack, following Cindy among the foot high fir seedlings. Douglas fir is an intolerant species, so it had to be harvested in one giant sweep, getting rid of the dense canopy that blocked sunlight and stopped a new stand.

Heartier than the seedlings, manzanita and fireweed

had grown quickly. Cindy stomped past a lush thicket full of red berries. Although I would have liked to pick some, I hustled after her.

"Seems like it must never rain up here. Everything's brown," I said.

"It rains," Cindy said. "But then it runs off too fast. Look." She bent over in that way I was learning to revere. "These things—the vetch and clover—they're great survivors. One's even called sweet-after-death."

She touched them as she had touched the dogs. Touching, I was glad to see, calmed her.

I know timber people argue that clear cutting is good for the wildlife. Makes more room for berries and herbs, affords a place in winter with lots of seeds for the little mammals. The man from the timber company stayed at Pilgrim's Harbor during the operation. He had a great speech about dwarf mistletoe and root rot, with clear cutting as the antidote to bad stand health. The poor guy had foot fungus so bad from the rain that fall, I could smell it in his room for months.

Cindy headed up a slash of stumps, already forgetting me, outpacing me by a quarter mile within ten minutes. I saw no reason to push yet, no reason not to keep a relaxed pace amid these beauties of nature.

Noises in a clear cut seem all wrong. There are no treetops to catch the wind, no places for birds, not even the echo of a stream. You imagine logging trucks and bulldozers, the grind of gears and slap of cables, diesel stress and the teeth of saws.

When I saw the deer, I nearly jumped out of my socks. It stood between us as Cindy turned along the ridge. It wasn't looking at either of us. It listened, scenting, but didn't flee.

I wondered if the deer might come over and eat from

my hand if I had a few nuts to offer. A blessing seemed to have come over us in the presence of this animal.

I looked at its ears, glad they didn't grow vertically—like rabbits'—but horizontally like a set of sleeves. Cindy hadn't seen it and walked on while I watched the deer evaluate its situation.

Not wanting to disturb it, but also not wanting to lose Cindy, I started to move slowly across the slash. A little Liszt in the background and the scene would make good Disney footage.

I caught sight of Cindy scrabbling uphill but then nearly tripped from the force of my sneeze. It was one of my violent, sudden explosions, half roar, half blast. I inherited the sneeze from my father, who used to brag about causing an elderly woman in the Lancaster train station to suffer a stroke when he erupted in the ticket line. I'm never at peace around weeds.

By the time I turned, I couldn't even see the deer's white tail. Its footfalls, however, were audible in the distance.

***

She sat with her back against a stump as big as the cab of a truck. Her knees were drawn up and hooped by her bare arms. The flannel shirt was now stuffed in her pack.

"I ought to swear off wood like I swore off meat," she muttered.

"Do you want to tell me what's bothering you? It's not like any of this should be a big surprise."

"You're absolutely right." There was a pause in which Cindy nestled more deeply into the dried ground cover. I scratched my back against a stump. "I shouldn't have called you."

"So you're not really available yet?"

"I'll probably never be available. It's the same old Cindy Bonds again. I've been in this town what, a month? Maybe three and a half weeks? And I'm already itching to leave. This is crazy."

I'd been sitting against the stump, but facing away from her. I rotated around it to touch Cindy's shoulder and could barely feel her beneath the layers of clothing.

"I thought you were getting settled."

"Just going through the motions." She leaned her head against my shoulder, then quickly moved it away. "Dewey, it seems that I don't settle very well and never have. All I can think about is where to go next."

She stood, folding her arms, putting more tree between us. There wasn't much to see up there. I knew she wasn't really looking.

"Can I help?"

"You know, when we met it seemed possible. It really did." She turned to look down at me. Finally, she was smiling, although it was without mirth. "This business about operating a motel, your being the professional accommodator. I thought you might be able to help me."

"What I thought was I might get to know you."

"I shouldn't have encouraged you."

I stood too. There was something about her assumption of control that both bothered me and rang true.

"No, you should just allow me to try."

I bent down, making a scooping motion above the leaves, and mimicked the packing of a snowball. I straightened and turned my back, smoothing the snowball while she stared. Then I whirled and threw it at her.

Cindy flinched. She wiped the side of her head where the snowball would have struck, nodded, and, in a gesture I hadn't seen her make before, slowly shut her eyes.

"You have a point," she said.

CHAPTER TWENTY

"See?" I asked when we'd settled down. "It has everything. Private table, view of the water, unobtrusive service. Just as advertised."

We'd come down from the clear cut to eat. Sullivan Reservoir is really a sunken forest. You can still look into it and see the tops of trees. Some even protrude above the surface in dry months.

We sat on the spillway rim with breakfast spread on an old towel. She called it breakfast; I'd call it forage.

She'd packed shredded wheat biscuits, to be eaten dry, a bag of something she called gorp, dried apricots, garbanzo beans with a dusting of hot spice. About the only thing she had that I'd ever eaten before was a chunk of cheddar, but the cheddar I've had was orange.

"If it's so nice," she said, "why aren't you eating?"

In answer, I chomped into the middle of a shredded wheat. It exploded and scattered fragments all over my lap.

"Let's get back to the game," I said. "It was your turn again."

We had been playing a modified version of the game she called Secrets. In the real version, each person in the group writes something about himself, something true, that he normally keeps as a secret. Then the Leader reads each secret and the group tries to guess whose it is.

The game, she said, is good for breaking barriers down among acquaintances. It's a bridge toward friendship.

I was all for crossing the bridge, but with two players we had to alter the rules. She thought a moment, swinging her feet above the water.

"You tell me a secret," she said. "It can be true or false. Then it's up to me to guess which."

"I go first?"

"Go ahead." She swallowed a fist of gorp and an apricot. I don't know how she could swallow anything after the shredded wheat without first having something to drink.

"I've lived in 18 different states," I said.

"False."

"No, that's true. One point, Howser."

"I'm impressed," she said. "I thought my nine was a lot."

"I don't have a college degree, though I always tell my employers I do."

"It's not your turn. But that's probably true."

"It shows?"

"No questions of the guesser. Now: I am not really living by myself. There's a man with me."

I stared at her with my mouth open. I reached in the bag of gorp, but kept the stuff in my hand.

"You're kidding!"

"True or false?"

"False. It has to be."

"Good. This game can be ruthless." She continued to eat with that old, abundant appetite. No wonder she was a runner. Otherwise she'd be a blimp. "In fact, it's best when it is."

"I lost my virginity at 21," I said.

"True."

"How'd you guess?"

"No cross-examination of the guesser, just of the guessee. I've already told you that. I go: I lost mine at 14."

I hesitated. "True."

"No. It's false."

"Then when?"

"None of your business."

"That's against the rules, isn't it?"

"Yes."

"Ok, if you're going to play mean: I was circumcised at age 27."

"Dear God, that must have been awful."

"It was."

"Gotcha. It's true."

"Nope. It's false." I leaned back and grinned. We weren't keeping score, but it seemed like I was winning.

"Ooo, very good. Here's one. I make a couple hundred bucks a year taking achievement tests for people. SAT, GRE, High School Equivalency. Law Boards cost you $500."

"True. You'd never make something like that up."

"False, but on a technicality. I charge a grand for the Law Boards. Are you going to keep avoiding the gorp?"

I put the gorp in my mouth and ground at it. It worked better to mash it like a horse does than to out-and-out chew.

"Delicious," I said when I could risk speaking. "I avoided the draft during Vietnam by claiming I was sole support of my widowed mother."

"You have no idea how special this gorp is. I make it myself, to my own secret proportions. Eat this and you'll never die. That's false, about the draft. They wouldn't take you because of bad teeth, or bad eyes, or a trick knee."

I nodded. "Heart murmur."

She began to clear up the meal and repack. "Last round, so it has to be personal. I have never been in love."

"True?"

"True."

"And I wouldn't know love if it hit me in the head."

"False."

"No, that's true."

"No, it isn't. You lose."

***

On the way back into town, we passed Dolfy Toskol running on the shoulder of the County Road and heading toward Pilgrim's Harbor. His wave included both of us.

I pulled off the road and got out to wait for him. We were still a good six miles from the motel, so he had to be pretty far along in mileage if he was in the back half of his run.

"I've got that Bug now," he said. Despite all his sweat, Toskol wasn't huffing. "This one's an 18 miler. Car will never catch me."

"I take it you don't want a ride to the motel?" I said.

He was running in place, scooting off to make little circles around my car, waving his arms, actually smiling. "No, but thanks for the offer."

"How's the race coming?" Cindy asked.

"Great. All set for the third, got the permit this morning."

"Any more entries?"

"We're up to seven now. I don't think I'm in trouble though. Two of the newcomers thought kilometers was a fancy name for miles and only signed up when I explained it wasn't a five miler."

Cindy smiled and leaned back against the car door. For an instant, I was afraid she was going to decide to run back with him.

"I think you'll be the top seed, Dolfy."

"Numbers! Oh, shit, I forgot to think about numbers. And safety pins! Dewey, would you consider hand-printing a couple hundred numbers, say 1 to 200, on squares of paper? You can print Pilgrim's Harbor Fourth of July Fun Run on top, for the free advertising."

"Why 200? You've only got seven runners."

"Same day sign ups. We'll have a crowd, you wait and see."

"Doesn't it bother you that the Fourth of July Fun Run is going to be on the third?"

"Nah," he said, starting to run off. "It doesn't matter if the date's accurate, just if the mileage is."

***

It was difficult to keep awake at work. That hardly ever happens to me. I even thought about calling in sick, which I've never done before, not even the time I had shingles.

When I dropped her off back at Westview Center, Cindy kissed me. She wouldn't let me see where she lived, but when I stopped by the front entrance to the mall she took my head in her hands. They were cool as she slipped them down along my jawline and then gently brought me closer. Her lips were very warm, though, and strong as they covered mine. Her tongue moved between my teeth and seemed enormous. She didn't just touch my tongue tip with hers, but laved the roof of my mouth, explored me, sought to touch wherever it could reach before leaving for the night.

In broad daylight.

"See you tomorrow," she said. She slammed the car door and disappeared into the mall.

I got to my apartment in time to shower, put on a change of clothes, and eat the peanut butter sandwich Cindy gave me because I hadn't eaten enough breakfast. The omens were becoming good: my missing X-acto knife and chisel turned up underneath the last towel in my closet.

It's a shame I was so tired, because there was a lot to do. Alla Mae had left an itemized list of everything she would need for the party and put neat red checks beside each one she found. There was a stack of receipts beside the list. Apparently, all she hadn't gotten hold of was an adequate supply of cherry Hi-C. I had to verify and reimburse.

Of course, since June is over, there's also the need to write my monthly summary for Jock Pruitt. He likes to have a feel for the specifics: how many guests each night, breakout of home states, check in and check out patterns. Busy work.

It would have been nice to find some quiet time to go through these things. But my first guest required my full attention.

Bennett Crow arrived excited and anxious to talk. He was driving home to Pittsburgh to attend his Uncle Millard's funeral and had been waiting years for opportunity.

"It's my turn," he said.

"You look healthy enough to me." I handed him the key to #19.

"This is great, this is just great. First, my Uncle William died up in New Hampshire. The whole family still lives in the east except me and two cousins. We live in California, as far away from home as we could get. So me and my cousins agreed that it didn't make sense to fly all three of us home for Uncle William's funeral. We chipped in and sent just one, my cousin Norman. I mean, my father came from a family of eight. They're all older than 75 and it's going to get expensive going back for each death."

"So it's your turn."

"Yeah. Two months after Uncle William died, Uncle Herman was killed crossing the street in Manhattan. Right away, we chipped in and sent my cousin Alex back. Alex had to fly first class because it was the holiday season and he couldn't get any other flight."

"OK, I can follow all that. So how come you're driving instead of flying?" I might not have asked, except I was so tired.

"Because I got a head start. Uncle Millard's not dead yet, but he can't possibly live out the week. Terminal renal disease. So I figure to drive home in a couple days, stay at some cheap joints like this, and then charge Norman and Alex first class round trip plane fare. They'll never know the difference. We don't bother with receipts."

He was too worked up to stand still. He left the office and turned the wrong way for his room. In a minute, he skipped past the door again and waved.

In quick succession, I had a microwave salesman who tried to sell me an oven for the office, two nuns who spoke German, a young couple heading to some Shakespeare festival, and a woman who had never been to the upper midwest.

I dozed in the recliner until Mike Strummer arrived. Good thing no one wanted a room after 9:00.

CHAPTER TWENTY-ONE

I didn't take my clothes off last night. Got to the apartment, collapsed onto the hide-a-bed, and slept until noon.

Couldn't remember any dreams. Just before I awoke, there was a vague, pleasant sense of growing lighter, of rising. The only problem I had this morning was that my hair stuck out like antlers.

For over thirty years, I've done my morning ablutions in the same order and at the same pace. But this morning, churning over the list of things I needed to get done, I rushed. That was how I discovered how difficult it is to eat an apple at the same time you take a shower.

I slowed down long enough to shave carefully, promising my reflection that I would begin the big cleanup tomorrow. But I don't anticipate order around here until after the holiday.

By the time I got to Pilgrim's Harbor, there had been two calls for me. Mike Strummer left the messages taped to the side of the registration cards, so I didn't see them for a while. I returned the calls in the order they came. It must have been a slow day at the police station since Delbert was in and was answering his own phone.

"Sorry I missed your call, but I was running a little late this morning."

"What do you know about this Dolfy Toskol character? Is he legit?"

"Who knows? All I can tell you is he hasn't been any trouble around here. Why?"

"Guy worries me. Suppose somebody ups and dies at this running race of his? Who pays if some fat old guy like me decides he's Alberto Salazar and pops a few valves? Seems hazardous to me."

"Toskol has that form everybody's got to sign. It says if you die it's nobody's damn fault but your own."

"You and me both know what good a piece of paper like that is. And also what's he doing messing around with our elected politicians? All the downtown people are haggling over who should shoot the starting gun and who gets to say 'ready, set, go'."

"He's just trying to get the whole town involved. I think that's consistent with the holiday spirit."

"Well, I made him give me a list of everybody who signed up to help. For security reasons. It's a regular who's who of this whole county. Except I don't see Dewey Howser's name on here anywhere."

"It's a morning event, Delbert. I was planning to be asleep at my apartment."

"You take my advice and be around. If it was my motel, I'd be damn sure I was there. This isn't a bake sale, kiddo, it's an insurance risk."

***

Before I returned the second call, Alla Mae came into the office. She wasn't exactly smirking, but I wouldn't call her expression a smile either. Bemused, maybe.

"You remember to order that cherry Hi-C?" she asked.

"Not yet. I just got in."

"You've been here almost 50 minutes. Anyhow, I already took care of it for you. This morning on the way to work. Here's your receipt."

She left, rattling the door a little more than she had to, and headed back for the rooms. What I could use is another dozen Alla Mae Buhls.

The second call had been from Lou Pumphrey. Talking to a dying man scares me, but not as much as failing to return his call. You don't want to offend these people.

"It's Dewey Howser, Mr. Pumphrey. I heard you wanted to talk to me."

"Did and do," he rasped. It hurt just to listen to him. "I figured if anybody knew about this Dolfy Toskol, it'd be his landlord. What can you tell me about the guy?"

"You too? Delbert Simmons just called asking the same thing. Why all the concern?"

"Well, we don't often have an outsider come in and stir things up like this. Besides, running's big these days and Toskol says we're way behind the rest of the country. He wants me to present the awards afterwards, like a guest of honor. The speech and the handshakes."

"You don't have to do that if you don't want to. Tell him you can't make it."

"Of course I want to. I love that kind of shit. Besides, the way he puts it, it's my civic duty. But he also wants me to get Creampuff Hambleton to spring for the trophies and I already hit The Puff for those flyers."

"I don't know what to tell you. Toskol certainly hasn't done anything suspicious around here. Too busy running."

"You don't think you could get Jock Pruitt to buy

some hardware for the winners? A little statue, a little medallion, maybe a coffee mug with the motel's name on it?"

"That's right, Mr. Pumphrey. I don't think I could get Jock Pruitt to do anything. If I were asking, it'd be for a raise."

"Well, that's about what I thought I'd hear, Howser." He sounded like a stereo when one of the speakers conks out. Volume suddenly falls and the tone is shot. "Easier to squeeze blood out of a turnip. Thanks for letting my daughter have the holiday. I'll see you at the race."

***

At 5:00, Cindy Bonds came walking into my office. She was carrying a small red suitcase. A purse was clutched in her left hand in lieu of the clunker she usually slung over her right shoulder.

The bell on my door hardly jingled. Cindy took a quick look around, the kind of glance meant less to assess the premises than to be sure we were alone.

"I'd like a room for the night, sir," she said.

I couldn't answer her. I simply stared. She looked ravishing.

Instead of that healthy, outdoor look she normally cultivated, Cindy had gone high-fashion. She wore heels, a thin dress that was mostly pale blue but had a pastel pattern of swirls, and a hoop of pearls around her neck. Her hair hung in wild ringlets.

"Don't tell me you have no vacancies," she said, with mock horror.

"I don't understand."

"That's true."

"I mean, what's this all about? There's trouble with your place or something?"

She walked closer to the counter and reached for my hand, which I'd abandoned beside the registration cards.

"It can be rather simple. Yesterday, for the first time in a long time, I had fun," she whispered. "I felt warm instead of cold. You made that happen."

"I'm glad."

"I've been alone and I don't always know what to do when someone actually likes me. When you wanted to be with me yesterday, I couldn't. Today, I can."

My pulse rate was soaring. She was talking to me in a way no one else ever had. I was surprised to find that I could understand the language.

I started to turn back to the rack of keys. But there was something that had to be said first.

"Cindy, I work here. Work. This is where I make my living."

"Not all night. When your shift is over, if you can break old habits, come to my room. I suppose you'll know how to find it."

I gave her #59. An end room.

***

A few minutes later, accompanied by a beast that would definitely be staying in the car tonight, Jay Ladue arrived. He was not what I expected of a campaign worker.

He did not now, nor did it seem likely that he ever would, look a day over 16. When he smiled, I saw that he had all of his teeth and half of someone else's. I would be surprised if he weighed more than 120 pounds, although he was a good six feet tall.

There was no place on his body for clothes to hang—no shoulders, no hips, no ass. The neck of his loose tee shirt looked ready to slip down over his left shoulder and his shorts threatened to bunch around his ankles like his socks had.

He should have pulled up on a Huffy utility bike with the newspaper bag over the handlebars, not in a new Buick. Coming barefoot and wet out of a pool, he'd leave no footprints.

How could a guy like this canvass a neighborhood or deal with a ward boss? How could he convince people to vote for his woman candidate?

Except that, immediately, I liked him. He inspired the impulse to trust. You couldn't help it; you could see before he spoke one word that this young man believed, absolutely and irrevocably, in the essential goodness of man.

Also, he was full of surprise and contradiction. For instance, his voice was an astonishing basso profundo, Henry Kissinger without the accent and charged with energy. It didn't seem possible that Ladue's frame could generate the required vibrations.

He was polite, but unstoppable as well. He knew what he wanted, knew his mission, and was not about to be denied.

"Professor Finfer sends his regards," Ladue said.

"How's the campaign going?"

"It's changing, that's for sure. The Professor says we've got it won already."

"There's nothing like confidence."

"I think he means that without the need for a party primary, there's no real contest. Not in Rhode Island. He can write her a lot of issue papers and it'll be just like school. Political science instead of politics."

Ladue looked down and noticed that his laces were untied. He disappeared below level of the counter and when he spoke, I could barely hear him.

"I would say that means we're dead meat."

He stood again, smiling. That's when I noticed about his teeth.

"What's that out in the car, a hippopotamus?"

"That's Maurice," Ladue said, scribbling something illegible on the registration card. "He's a French mastiff. Maurice won't hurt you."

"That's right, because I'm not going to be anywhere near him."

"Don't sweat it. He sleeps in the car. I'll just take him for a run twice a day and he'll be fine."

I was glad Ladue didn't need to be told about dogs in the room. Since he mentioned running, I told him about Dolfy Toskol and the race tomorrow.

"I might stay for it," he said, "unless the Professor, once I go through his stuff, wants me to get there in a hurry."

"OK, let me get you the briefcase."

Ladue followed back behind the counter and into my office. I hadn't expected that.

His eyes went carefully over every surface of the room. I couldn't help feeling chilled, as if he were checking to see if I'd left any of the documents lying around while I was sneaking a read. Or maybe he was memorizing the layout.

The briefcase was under the walnut table, looking from the distance like a matching piece of furniture. It was upright and locked.

I was relieved that Mike Strummer had left it alone. I'd never mentioned the briefcase to him, hoping he'd fail to notice it during his late-night and early-morning stint, or if he did, that he'd be unwilling to risk offending me.

I reached for it, but Ladue was right beside me and snagged it first. He had no trouble hefting it, which surprised me since it weighed so much.

"Thanks, Mr. Howser. You've been a great help." He staggered a little leaving the room and shifted the briefcase to his left hand.

"My pleasure."

"Now I'd like to take this to the room and spend some time putting things in order. The Professor wants me to call at midnight, Rhode Island time. He wants some information real bad."

CHAPTER TWENTY-TWO

It was hectic until 10:00, when the last room was taken. People were getting a head start on the holiday traffic and most of the guests were gripped in the iron hand of travel dementia. They saw nothing but the road, cared for nothing but its end, spoke of nothing but route numbers and miles and states to go.

At one point, I actually had a queue. Desk to door, there were nine people lined up. Through the door, I could count several more until I lost sight of them beyond the range of the lights.

It was as noisy as the lobby of a theater at intermission. As smoky, too, since most of them ignored my No Smoking signs. This was a night when even I could see they'd earned their smokes.

These are hardly the conditions in which you get to know the guests. It's rush rush, sign them up and give them the key, efficiency is all.

Process them.

It's difficult to do my best work this way. I can't get to know the guests, to evaluate their situations and give them the room that's best suited to their needs. If it were always like this, I might as well be at a Holiday Inn in downtown New York and make some big cash.

By 11:00, it was over. The NO was turned on, the records were in order, and the guests were reasonably quiet. None of tonight's guests seemed like the kind that would prowl the grounds, spend a few hours at Harbor Side, or cruise through town looking for a drink. They were focused on tomorrow's mileage.

I took my normal closing stroll through the parking lot just before midnight. Mike Strummer should be here soon. I noticed that the light was still on in #59.

***

I left the office as usual, saying good-night to Strummer and turning away from the rooms. Then I circled the motel office and walked unseen to #59. This was another advantage of an end room.

I tapped on the door with my fingertips, hoping Cindy would be awake. In a few seconds, she opened the door.

"I could have been a prowler," I said, slipping inside the room.

"Maybe, but I watched you leave the office so I was comfortable that it was you. Besides, I know tae kwon do."

"Me too. I think he stayed here once."

Her dress was draped over a chair. Her red suitcase was against the wall beneath the painting of a clipper ship and her shoes were neatly aligned in front of it. She wore a satiny black robe that offered stark contrast to her hair.

On the bed, face-down, was a book she'd been reading. It was called *Dinner at the Homesick Restaurant*. Sounds like my kind of book. On the table beside the bed, she'd put a portable tape player which emitted a soft, bluesy guitar.

"Come here, Dewey."

I obeyed. She took my face in her hands again and kissed me. It was a more leisurely kiss this time, good-natured, with a grin behind it.

"You smell smoky," she said.

"It was a madhouse tonight. They were so daffy, I'm surprised they could remember their own names and addresses. I didn't have the heart to stop them."

"Why don't you take a shower? I hear this motel has endless hot water and Ivory soap. You'll feel better."

"I don't know how I could feel much better, but I'd love to take a shower."

When I began to walk toward the bathroom, Cindy put a hand on my arm. She pulled me back and wrapped her arms around me from behind.

"Poor, naive Dewey."

She tugged my shirt up and over my head. She unbuckled my belt, then ran her warm hands up my back and through my hair.

"Now go on," she said, pushing me gently toward the bathroom.

She had put a bottle of shampoo on the window ledge inside the shower. I lathered up, rinsed, and leaned back against the wall to let the warm spray work on me. Gradually, the sense of urgency left me. It faded and was gone, like the soapiness in the water I watched disappear down the drain.

I shut off the water. A thick towel hung over the top of the shower, which she must have put there while I wasn't looking. When I opened the bathroom door, its warmth and moisture rolled with me into the room. It was darker than it was before.

There was now a strong scent of anise. She'd lit a candle and shut off the overhead light. Only the lamp above her head was on. When I emerged, she shut it off. Despite the flickering light of the candle, I could see her clearly, as if my vision had suddenly sharpened.

I remember thinking, Maybe this is possible. Maybe this is really happening. I never believed that the truly beautiful women, the women like Cindy Bonds who could make you stop worrying about the impact of time, were available to me.

***

At first, I was afraid I would lose control. I was afraid I wouldn't be able to keep gentleness in my passion for her, that I'd hurt her.

Of course, for all my admiration of her form, I'd forgotten the strength it implied. She went at me as hungrily as she went at her food up at the reservoir.

When I reached the bed, Cindy rose on her knees and undid the belt of her robe. It opened slightly, caught beneath her knees and on her breasts.

I slipped my hands between the robe and her skin, nudging the robe off her shoulders. She lay back down. Freed from the weight of her body, the robe fell open.

It must have been clear that I was holding myself

back, gathering control like a downhill skier in the starting chute. She lifted her chin very slightly, a beckoning. I understood that the first need was to kiss.

Wordlessly, eyes closed, she showed me that kisses had the power to explore as well as yield. Then she did the same with her hands. I wasn't in a hurry, but I wanted to find out what would happen next.

"Motels," she whispered.

"But it's not just any motel." I rested my cheek against the point of her shoulder and my nose was beneath her ear. We were getting close. "This is my place."

After a while, Cindy shifted weight and moved a few inches away. We were finished talking.

She kissed my chest, licked down one ridge of the hair that runs from there to my groin but stopped just below my navel. Then she licked back up.

If the sheets were silk, they could not have been more slick than we made them. It was warm. What we did was mostly new to me. But Cindy knew enough to know what she liked, to show me without seeming to instruct. When we were finished, lying together half-asleep, I understood what it might mean to lose yourself.

CHAPTER TWENTY-THREE

There was no way that I could stay the night.

I had to go back to my apartment. That was where my day had to begin.

The idea of emerging from #59 in daylight, of being seen by Mike Strummer, or by anyone for that matter, was unacceptable. I know what I would have thought seeing Strummer leave a guest's room in the pre-dawn hours.

It seemed clear to me that my life, both its outer

skin and its inner substance, had become endangered. It was like a helium balloon floating up there above me and I had better hold tight if I didn't want it to get away.

Cindy understood. In fact, she suggested that I leave.

"I've got a race in the morning," she said.

Sometime between 4:00 and 4:30, I kissed the back of her neck, dressed as quietly as I could, and slunk from the room. Part of me felt like leaping up and clicking heels in the darkness. Most of me, however, opted for furtive escape.

If it had been me in the office when the car started up, I'd have gone to the window to check out the noise. I don't think Mike Strummer did. I'd be surprised if he was awake.

There were four and a half hours until The Pilgrim's Harbor Fourth of July Fun Run. If I allowed myself to sleep, chances were that I wouldn't get up in time or if I did, that I'd be too woozy to be of any use.

After another shower, this one as necessary but not as sensuous as the earlier one, my inclination was to carve. It would be nice to have the reality of wood in hand.

Besides having found the X-acto knife and chisel, I'd also located the missing sandpaper and the gouge I'd given up on. In the top of the closet—not lost but not expected to be used again—was my horde of white pine, cypress, and larch chunks. Carving seemed worth a try.

I sat down on the hide-a-bed, put a magazine in my lap, and began to sketch. When I'm roughing out a project, I use graph paper with one inch squares to lay out a scale drawing. Some people can carve without sketches, but that's not for me. I need the plans.

After working on a few undistinguished heads, I switched to the kind of standing figure that I can do almost automatically. When that didn't lead anywhere, I drew a bell that looked more like a flying saucer. Then I quit. At least I'd finally gotten all my carving tools together.

Then it came to me. I should bake bread for Cindy.

To strengthen my hands, was what she had said. I wonder if she still thinks my hands need strengthening.

In a recent issue of *Mobile Home Life* that a guest had left behind, there were recipes for breads that could be made on the road. I'd brought the issue home because it contained an article on out-of-the-way spots to eat that mentioned Henri's.

I've never attempted to make bread. Like most people, I never seriously considered that modern man, as opposed to large companies with cheerful names, retained the capacity to do it. Therefore, it hadn't occurred to me, until I read the recipe, how many ingredients are involved in a simple loaf of bread.

I took stock. There was some flour around because I had once tried and failed to fry chicken. It was white instead of whole wheat, but I didn't think that would really matter.

There was also yeast. Earlier this year I'd bought a package by mistake, thinking it was a trial-size sample of laundry powder.

Oil, water, salt, milk: no problem. Honey, wheat germ, and rolled oats might be trouble, though.

Since Cindy had said she had a sweet tooth, I figured substituting sugar for honey would be all right. It might even enhance the taste for her.

Wheat germ was an item I'd never dealt with. It was

difficult to imagine that the bread would miss a measly half cup of wheat germ. But I didn't want to take any chances. It seemed as if leaving one thing out altogether might make the whole enterprise collapse.

So I shook a bunch of Wheaties into a bag and pounded on them until they were well crushed. The texture seemed about right for something called wheat germ.

In the pantry there were several envelopes of instant oatmeal, the kind you just add boiling water to. It didn't amount to three cups, but I figured it might expand when I put in the water.

When I had all my ingredients assembled, there were a little over three hours left to kill. Dewey Howser was making bread!

When Cindy said oatmeal bread was sticky, she wasn't kidding. Within five minutes, the dough was everywhere. My watchband was caked with it, splatters adhered to the cabinets and the floor, and I didn't see how I'd ever get it out from under my fingernails. People eat this stuff?

Eventually, I got it into one piece that I could extract my fingers from with relative ease. I set the bowl aside to let the dough rise. It felt warm enough in the kitchen so that, as long as there wasn't a draft, I thought it should work.

An hour later, the dough seemed to have spread rather than risen. I figured "rise" was just a semantic issue, a cookbook term for "expand" or "grow." So I punched it like the recipe said, cut it in half, rolled each into a loaf, and stuffed them into empty coffee cans that had the lids removed.

The rest, I figured, was out of my hands. After about a half hour, I popped the cans into the oven and let the loaves bake the required forty-five minutes.

Well, say forty minutes, give or take. Time was running out.

I didn't bother to take the loaves out of their cans. I just wrapped them, hot and fresh, in my only two clean dish towels. Then I ran down to the car with them. They smelled alive and sweaty.

While I'd waited for the bread to finish rising, I realized it wasn't going to be possible to get to Pilgrim's Harbor by 8:15, when I'd told Dolfy Toskol I'd be there to help with the start of the race. I hoped it would begin a little late.

Alongside the road, I noticed that fluorescent orange numbers had been spraypainted every half mile or so. Toskol had measured and marked the course. I don't know how he got permission from the Mayor.

At 8:45, when I arrived at the motel, the parking lot was nearly as full as it had been last night. But most of the license plates were from here.

A red, white, and blue banner was strung from the carport to the roof of the office. FIRST ANNUAL PILGRIM'S HARBOR FOURTH OF JULY FUN RUN. Delbert was perched on a stepladder, a bullhorn to his mouth, issuing orders no one seemed to be heeding.

I parked on the shoulder of the road. There were people everywhere.

CHAPTER TWENTY-FOUR

It was clear at a glance that, among the 200 or so people who had assembled, all but about a dozen were spectators. Most were dressed for a parade, many had on their Sunday clothes, a few had cameras and binoculars slung around their necks, and none had on running shoes.

They milled around, chatting, looking for the actual runners. Lou Pumphrey, dressed for January weather, and his friend Creampuff Hambleton had Gilliam off to one side. Gilliam, the kid who works at Harbor Side, looked like he'd been eating too many of the customers' leftovers. He was doing knee bends and nodding at the ex-ballplayers' advice.

Nearer to me, gripping the side of Delbert's stepladder, was Dolfy Toskol. He wore the shorts, kneepads, and hat that he always wore. But something about him looked different.

It was his shirt. The thing was a flagrant pink and turquoise nylon, with cut-off sleeves and a scooped neck. It reminded me of a jockey's silks. But it was also more than his shirt.

Now that I moved next to him, I noticed that he had a watch on each wrist, wristbands above the watches, and a headband worn so low on his forehead that it made his ears stick out. He was leaning hard against the ladder, stretching his legs, and Delbert was looking down on him with genuine concern.

"This piece of equipment's none too steady, pal," Delbert said. "Why don't you lean up against that nice building over there to do your stretching instead?"

"Hello, Dewey." Toskol said. He didn't move.

"Sorry I'm late. Bread in the oven."

"That's one I've never heard before," Delbert said, letting out the band on his Mariners cap. The mark it left on his forehead was so deep, I thought it might eventually meet the mark from the back of his hair somewhere at the center of his brain.

"No problem," Toskol said. "Plenty of volunteers around to get everything set up."

"Anything I can do now?" I asked.

"No. You just enjoy it. Put your money on me, though. I feel fleet today."

"I've got an idea," Delbert said. "Why don't you ride in the car with me, Dewey? That way you can watch the race, be the first one back to the motel at the end, and keep an eye on things."

I agreed. It would be good to have something to do and fun to ride in a cop car.

"Ten minutes to race time," Delbert bellowed through the bullhorn. "All you spectators move on out from the starting area please."

I spotted Cindy in front of Room #59. She had on a pink sweat suit and was bending over to touch her toes. Her hair was yanked back tightly and hung down in a pony tail.

She was talking to someone who was lying on the ground with both legs flung back over his shoulders. His toes touched ground behind his head.

As I approached, I could see that Cindy also had on a pink and white cloth headband. She looked comfortable and happy, a mood I hoped was in part my doing.

The person on the ground unfolded. It was Jay Ladue. So he'd decided to stay for the race.

"Professor Finfer said I could take my time. That was all I needed to hear." He smiled at me, all tooth, and then turned the beam toward Cindy.

"Jay's quite the runner," she said. "Collegiate star, 2:30 marathoner, free shoes from Nike."

"I keep telling Cindy all that was years ago. I'm afraid I'm just an old, out of shape runner now." He smiled some more. I didn't believe a word of it. "That's what politics does to you."

He began to strip off his warmup gear, still sitting

on the ground. I would have thought he could simply shrug out of them, but he approached it more as a solemn ritual.

He worked his sweat pants slowly over his racing shoes and flung them aside, then unzipped his shirt. Underneath was the skimpiest pair of shorts that I've ever seen. They were cut all the way up his thigh so that they didn't seem to connect at the waist. He also had on a shirt with almost no sides to it, just shoulder straps, and a front and back that merged somewhere inside his shorts.

He was entirely too close to naked. My first impression had been correct: the man was without buttocks.

Then Cindy peeled off her warmup gear too. It was strange. Here, last night, I'd slept with her but hadn't seen her undress. Watching her now was deeply arousing to me.

At the same time, coming as it did just after Ladue had stripped down, her actions seemed like an erotic response to his. I tried not to consider that. Instead, I noticed that she wore a matched black and burgundy racing outfit that had a New Balance logo. Where'd she get that, from Salvo? Her full breasts, which I couldn't help but notice, were bound tight by some sort of monster bra.

It wasn't possible to say anything personal or private to Cindy. I wished them luck and walked away.

On the way back to Delbert and Dolfy Toskol, I passed Mel Salvo, the salesman from Westview Center. He would walk a few steps, then take off at a sprint for ten yards, jog to a stop, and repeat the process coming back. His hair was also tied in a pony tail.

***

All in all, Dolfy Toskol had managed to sign up 14 racers. The $70 in entry fees just covered expenses, with $4 left over toward the second annual run next year. It was a good thing, Toskol said, that most of what he needed for the race had been donated.

Mayor Franklin Crawford, who is Lou Pumphrey's cousin, made a brief speech thanking Jock Pruitt for sponsoring the race. He thanked Delbert Simmons for donating his time. He thanked God for this great country of ours, which we were honoring with this wonderful event as part of its birthday celebration, and he reminded all concerned that running represented freedom and that freedom was what this holiday was all about.

It wasn't bad. And he did it in less than a minute.

"Don't anybody start running until Mr. Pruitt shoots that pistol," Delbert said through his bullhorn.

With that, his duties on the stepladder were over. He left the bullhorn on the platform and dismounted slowly, making the ladder shudder.

We got into his car. I rolled down my window and leaned out. Mike Strummer waved from where he was standing in the office doorway. He was still in charge of the motel.

Jock Pruitt climbed the stepladder, lugging a small tape recorder with him. He picked up the bullhorn, put the recorder on the top step and turned it on, then put the bullhorn up against the speaker.

If you strained and sorted out the feedback, you could tell that it was the National Anthem. The 14 runners straightened to listen respectfully, bouncing up and down.

When it was over, the crowd cheered. The runners stood under the banner—seven runners in front, seven behind—and reached for their watches.

Jock Pruitt's shot misfired. There was a brief discussion between Pruitt and his wife at the bottom of the ladder. The runners, grumbling, got reorganized. Pruitt yelled "GO" and they took off.

***

Delbert flicked on the revolving lights and the siren. He pulled out of the driveway, turned west, and floored it. I looked out of the back window.

"Slow down, Delbert. You're losing them."

Gilliam had sprinted into the lead. But by the time he reached the County Road he'd pulled over to the shoulder and stopped, bent over with his hands on his knees, looking hard into the weeds.

We turned the corner onto the road and I lost sight of the runners briefly. Then they came into view.

First around was Dolfy Toskol, a huge smile on his face. His head was flung back and his legs splayed out side to side.

A little ways back, running easily side by side and talking, were Jay Ladue and Cindy. He seemed to be pacing her. He glided, feet hardly hitting the ground. She glided too, though with a kind of larger motion, an eagle rather than a dove.

It was a long time before anybody else turned the corner. We were too far ahead to see who it was.

Just before the big orange 2 on the side of the road, there was a card table set up. In front of it were the maids from Pilgrim's Harbor and behind it was Alla Mae, filling dixie cups with water.

I waved when we drove by. Alla Mae nodded once, almost like a sneeze, then went back to her chores.

Dolfy Toskol, still in the lead, grabbed a cup and tried to drink. Most of the water splashed out before it reached his lips. He flung the cup aside. Delbert hadn't seen that or he might have ticketed him for littering.

The race was going as Toskol had wanted it to until we turned back onto the frontage road. There was a half-mile to go. He looked over his shoulder to assess his lead, looked forward quickly as if to be sure we were watching too, looked back again, and then opened his mouth in an enormous O.

Effortlessly and rapidly, Jay Ladue was catching Dolfy Toskol. Not only that, Cindy was right beside him, strain etching her face. She was trying to catch Toskol too.

"I can't watch," I said.

"I can," Delbert patted the rearview mirror. "That Toskol character's gonna lose. He-he. He's not only gonna lose to the wimp, he's gonna lose to the cooze." He took a peek back. "He-he."

I closed my eyes.

***

"I faded, Dewey. Went out too quick."

Dolfy Toskol was inconsolable. He sat slumped against the side of the office, drinking something the color of moss. Sweat cascaded down his face and neck.

He had planned to win. He was so certain of his victory that he'd only arranged for one trophy—winner take all.

"Still, you picked up a lot of miles on the car," I said. "It hasn't been a total loss."

Toskol's disappointment moved me more than the joy their side by side victory brought Ladue and Cindy.

It had seemed cruel to me. Certainly Cindy knew how much the race meant to Toskol, even if Ladue didn't.

At the finish, Ladue had grabbed Cindy's left hand and steered her across the line. She was staggering a little, obviously near exhaustion. He made sure they finished in a tie.

Then she'd turned toward him and fallen into his arms. I had two reactions at once: 1) I was sure she'd knock the guy over. 2) If she didn't knock him over, I wanted to.

Enough of that.

I think I'm getting a little run down.

Not enough sleep, too much excitement, too much going on.

After the last runner finished, it took less than an hour to clean up the parking lot and remove all traces of the race. We drove out on the course to fetch the cups and bring in Alla Mae and her troops. We rolled the banner up and stored it in the office closet in case there really is a race next year.

Mike Strummer went home a little early, since I was already around. He'd taken two rolls of pictures, mostly of the spectators.

Well before the noon deadline, Cindy checked out. She was elated, her face flushed either from the race or the shower. I'd seen her that flush once before, last night, but it was between and across her breasts.

Ladue had given her the trophy which they jointly won and she wanted me to see it. Yes, she'd had a wonderful night, thank you, and now a wonderful morning. She felt that things were looking up.

I didn't think to give her the bread. I never really had a chance.

A few minutes after Cindy left, Dolfy Toskol walked

into the office. He smiled, shook my hand, and gave me a $25 check to cover a gift for Alla Mae's team. He was dressed in traveling clothes, not running clothes.

"I never do a training run the same day I race," he explained. "How far is it to the next motel?"

"Thirty miles."

"Jesus. Car's going to close the gap. Maybe I'll stay there a few days and get in some twenty mile runs."

Then he was gone.

At noon, Ladue came to the office. He was emptyhanded.

"I'm in no rush to leave," he said. "Besides, I hear you're having a big party tomorrow. I'll stay through to the fifth, OK?"

What was I going to do, throw him out?

CHAPTER TWENTY-FIVE

The Hazelriggs arrived at 3:30. I'd expected a convoy. I'd expected Jerome Hazelrigg to be a huge man, probably a farmer, and to have huge children with hair like Kansas cornstalks and bodies like barns.

Since the evening of June 30th, I've been expecting them to bring trouble.

Jerome and Rachel, the parents, were driving together in a sleek Firebird. The girls, Naomi, Janet, Paula, and Monica, were right behind them in an old Impala. The boys, Clarence and Alvin, were twins and were driving the new Subaru. They didn't arrive until 5:00.

Hazelrigg is an accountant; his wife teaches biology at Washburn. The boys live at home. They operate the family's small catering business. Naomi is a physician and Janet is going to be. Paula and Monica are still in school.

So what I have here is a close-knit, solid, and reasonably well-to-do midwestern family. They arrange their lives to assure a long vacation together every summer. When they swam in the pool, the boys brought towels for everyone, the girls brought suntan lotion, the parents stayed in their room.

Nothing bad's going to happen.

***

Julian Mills wasn't used to being up during the day. When he checked in at 4:30, he was wired on caffeine. His breath reeked of coffee, his eyes didn't blink, and he talked so fast I could hardly understand him.

"Hacker."

"Julian Hacker?"

"No, Mills. Hacker's what I do. Am, I mean. Computers. At night. I sleep all day. This is killing me."

"Why don't you travel at night?"

"Can't see well enough. Screen strain."

The door opened behind him. Mills screeched, zipping to the corner of the room. He stared at a woman and her toddler who'd just pulled in.

"Jesus," he said. "I'm a bat; what's the price for a rafter?"

He left, watched carefully by little Sammy Maxwell. The child, who had just mastered walking by himself, turned to me and giggled. I guess he liked the way Mills moved.

It was good to be getting back into the rhythm of things. Pilgrim's Harbor was filling up. My kind of people were on the road today, it seemed. I was losing myself again in the world that I best understood.

Melissa Maxwell wanted a roll-away for Sammy.

"He's out of the crib at home. I'd hate to put him back in one."

I gave it to her at no extra charge.

***

The moon was up early. It was getting cool, a welcome break from the stuffy office.

I watched two figures approaching from the direction of downtown. One glided, the other—Maurice the mastiff—lumbered. Back inside, I realized that my schedule was all confused. Now I was hungry, which comes from sleeping when I was supposed to be eating. I couldn't remember the last time I'd gone to the bathroom.

All I had handy to eat was the bread, Cindy's bread. I'd forgotten to bring anything with me for my evening meal and couldn't afford Harbor Side yet this month.

I brought one loaf in, unwrapped it, and tried to remove it from the can. No luck.

The crust, which I expected to be rock hard, was spongy. When I tried to force the loaf out, my fingers sunk in. The only option was to pinch out a piece at a time.

This bread, this token of affection, could be chewed but it couldn't be swallowed.

***

At 9:00, Cindy Bonds showed up. I saw her walk along the driveway, led by Abelard on his blue nylon leash. She didn't stop, or look inside. They passed underneath the carport and went toward the rooms.

I walked out after her. Cindy heard my door open and turned.

"Hello, Dewey. I'm really getting to know my way around this place, aren't I?"

"This is a surprise. You should have come in."

"I didn't want to disturb you." Her voice went flat. She sounded disappointed that I was around.

Where did she think I'd be? I mean, this is my motel. She had to know I'd see her.

"Actually, I was hoping you'd come by," I said. "Why didn't you call?"

"I did call. And Jay said he was free. We're going to take our dogs for a walk."

She looked away. The expression on her face was difficult to read in the darkness. It might have been pain; it could have been impatience.

"Jay?"

"Jay Ladue. I met him this morning at the race, remember? It turns out we have a lot in common."

"And it turns out you're going to see him now."

"That's right." She picked Abelard up and held him in her arms like a child. "I know what you're thinking, Dewey. I was afraid you might be this way—that was my only hesitation about last night."

"This way?"

"Attached. Possessive." The dog squirmed, so she put him down. "Last night was something I wanted to do last night. It was my choice. But it's not what I want to do every night."

"You're going a little fast for me, Cindy. I don't remember saying anything about every night. All I remember saying is I hoped you'd come by tonight."

"I told you about me before, you know." The brittleness in her voice was worse than the nastiness that day in front of Westview Center. "I warned you that I don't settle."

I felt like I was choking. When she finished speaking, it was like someone had socked me in the back trying to dislodge a chunk of meat and made it get stuck worse. I tried to breathe deeply, to relax.

"I wasn't thinking settle. I was thinking care."

Cindy shook her head. She raised her right hand, palm outward, and froze it in the universal signal for Stop.

I moved a step toward her. Or maybe I didn't. We seemed a little closer than when she'd put up her hand. It was an illusion, I suppose. She wasn't closer, just clearer to the eye.

Her sadness, or what I took to be her sadness, seemed to rise up between us like a breaker. It was a threatening thing. But it was my own unacknowledged sadness, not hers. It swamped me like a wave.

As I backed toward the door, I understood that this had not come simply because of Cindy's cavalier attitude toward the connection I thought we'd made. It was my seeing, as if in a mirror held out in her palm, all that was missing from my life.

CHAPTER TWENTY-SIX

Forget it.

***

What is more inevitable, that a guest arrive or that a guest leave?

You knew all along how this business worked, Howser.

***

Warm today, with a threat of thunderstorms.

***

A month has gone by. As I look back on that Fourth of July, memory may play a few tricks with me. The day probably didn't happen just as I remember it now. I'm ready to give it a try.

***

I awoke at about 9:00, sheets asunder, perspiring like Dolfy Toskol after the race. The dream escaped me, but I sat up recalling its final image of Maurice standing over me where I lay. His fawn colored face was an inch from mine. He was shaking with rage, moisture from his dewlaps drenching me, oval eyes riveted on my shut eyes waiting for them to open so I could see what would then destroy me.

Although I had no appetite, I forced myself to eat a bowl of cereal and a banana. I left the apartment without bothering to fold up the hide-a-bed.

When I got to Pilgrim's Harbor, Alla Mae was genuinely excited. She had three tables already set up at the far side of the pool. One was covered with a red tablecloth, a second was covered by a white bedsheet, and the third had what appeared to be blue contact paper on it.

A carton of fireworks was stashed under the blue table. There was an aluminum tub beneath the white table, the sort that people used to soak their tired feet in, and Alla Mae was kneeling by it lining up various bottles. I'd never seen her look so content.

"You've got to mix this stuff up in advance," she said when I neared. "Let it steep, sort of."

"This looks wonderful," I said, though without enough enthusiasm to satisfy her.

"Best I could do." She turned back to her work. "Especially short-handed."

I went into my office. Mike Strummer had picked up the room a little for the holiday, taken Windex to the glass, refilled the brochure rack. He'd even run a fresh pot of coffee through the machine before leaving.

It wasn't going to be possible to find out if Cindy had spent the night in Ladue's room unless I asked Strummer, who probably wouldn't know. I certainly wasn't going to ask Alla Mae, who cleaned it up, or Ladue, who walked in smiling.

"Professor Finfer revised the schedule again," he said. "I hope this won't be too inconvenient, my changing plans all the time."

"I'm flexible." I must have been smiling back at him.

"Good. Then we'll leave this afternoon. I don't think I can make the noon deadline, though. I hope you won't charge me extra."

"Just try not to mess up the room too much. Alla Mae hates to clean twice."

"No problem there. I've already run and showered. All I have to do is pack and write a little report for the Professor on the campaign's spending plan. It's Cindy that's the delay. I don't think she'll be packed till about sundown."

Now here's where my memory gets a little fuzzy. The news was no more than I'd come to expect. I recollect a long silence, Ladue watching me closely, the sense of coffee acids underneath my tongue.

"She's going with you," I said.

"It was a long-shot, but I thought I'd ask. This is amazing." He began to count off points on his fingers. "She's always wanted to see the east coast, she's always wanted to be involved in a political campaign, especially for a female candidate, and she was more than ready to leave here. I found a place for her dog last night and we're set. Who'd ever have guessed I'd luck into this?"

"Congratulations," was the best I could do.

"Thanks. Say, could you give me an extra plastic bag? My running gear's wet and I don't like to pack it with the rest of my things."

***

The Hazelriggs offered to help with the party preparations. They had lots of snacks that could be donated, a case of pop in the girls' trunk. Jerome said he was handy with the banjo and Rachel knew thousands of songs.

"We could probably get the kids to organize a square dance, too," he said.

I tried to be polite, to accept their offer with grace. "Seeing as how you're practically tenants."

As the day wore on, however, my attitude shifted. I began to see the Hazelriggs as a burden, to distrust their intentions, and to worry about the damage they were planning to inflict. They hadn't gone anywhere since checking in. They just sat around the pool, or in each other's rooms. They played board games and loyally gathered to watch the twins dive.

But I didn't like the looks of things. Worse than harming the rooms would be insulting the guests, creating a scene that would ruin Pilgrim's Harbor. As the day wore on, I began to be certain that was their plan.

In this way, obsessed with the impending calamity of the Hazelriggs, I was able to nudge Cindy Bonds from my mind. All afternoon, I avoided looking toward Ladue's room in case I should see her arrive. I stalked around Pilgrim's Harbor in a frenzy of concern.

CHAPTER TWENTY-SEVEN

I didn't see Cindy arrive. That's why I don't know how long she watched me carrying on.

She must have seen me bouncing from the pool area to my office to the Hazeleriggs' rooms to the edge of the lot where their cars were parked out of the way. She must have waited until I came to rest alone in my office before deciding it was time to walk in.

She didn't say anything right away. It seems to me now that she was sizing up the situation. Then, I thought she was being unkind.

"I know you're leaving," I said into her silence. "Your boyfriend told me."

"Dewey, I'm sorry." She inhaled deeply, trying to remain sympathetic. "Jay's not my 'boyfriend.' He's someone I know a little and I'm fond of him."

"If this is what you're willing to do when you're fond of somebody, what happens when you're in love?"

I expected her to be angry. It would have been easier, as a matter of fact, if she stormed out. I don't think I believed too much in the moral position behind what I was feeling, anyway.

"What happened between you and me happens all the time. What's happening now happens all the time." She started to open the door to leave, then stopped herself. She had more to say. "You should wake up, Dewey. It's the 1980s."

"I knew that."

How we got from there to the kiss, I can't say. She kissed me, though, and held me for a long time with

her strong arms around my back.
And goodbye.

***

At 6:00 sharp, as promised, Mike Strummer came through the door. If he was surprised at what I looked like, I don't remember that he let it show.

Later, I heard he'd almost called for help. Apparently, I'd been sick and hadn't done a very good job cleaning up.

At 6:30, Strummer lit the first of the skyrockets. All the guests had come out to the pool and by then were formed into groups, deep into their discussions of travels and homes. They stopped when the pinwheel took off and applauded its display.

It was a hot, humid night. I was the only person not in shorts. I don't own a pair of shorts.

Jerome Hazelrigg spotted me and waved. At his signal, one of the daughters brought me a can of beer. Although I don't drink on the job, I drank on the job.

I remember snippets of conversation.

Monica Hazelrigg was a sophomore.

Jerome Hazelrigg would like me to come to his room later and join him for a real drink. He thought this party was a wonderful gesture.

Naomi is a pediatrician but Janet wants to be a gynecologist.

A couple from the Upper Peninsula had driven nine hundred miles today, exactly 450 each.

Jock Pruitt thought this party was a great idea after all. He'd have something for me in the morning.

Someone from North Carolina was also named Dewey. Only he spelled his D-u-e-y. He wondered whether that wasn't funny?

Alla Mae thought the embalming fluid was practically perfect.

Children should be allowed to stay up as late as they wanted.

Delbert Simmons was glad I had everything under control.

***

I gradually drifted away from the party. Once Jerome Hazelrigg got out the banjo, and Rachel began to sing along with him, spirits around the pool really began to lift. It was a pleasant gathering before; it was a festival now. The various smaller groups began to merge.

No one missed me. I found myself in the far corner of the parking lot, where the Hazelriggs had left their cars.

They seemed like the sort of people who would be careful to lock their car doors. Accountant, professor, professional kids. But I assume they felt safe at Pilgrim's Harbor. At any rate, the doors were unlocked.

I know what I was thinking when I opened the Subaru. If these people were planning any disruption, the boys would be the ones to carry it out. I told myself I was looking for contraband, looking for drugs, explosives, looking for the makings of trouble.

There was nothing unusual inside. Maps of the states they'd been in, a case of tapes for the stereo, a stash of chewing gum. The car was neater than my living room.

The parents' Firebird had the most junk in it, but nothing sinister. Apparently, they were in the habit of tossing candy wrappers, empty paper cups, McDonald's containers, and the daily newspaper in the unoccupied back seat. Judging from the bottom layer of papers, they hadn't cleaned the car since March.

I can see now that I was lost. Monica, the sophomore, had followed me toward the cars because she wanted to get me to sing.

When she saw me ratting through the Subaru, she must have run back and gotten her parents. By the time they came back, I was on my hands and knees in the back seat of the girls' Impala.

***

What was I doing?

I know I wasn't looking for a bomb, like I told Jock Pruitt when he arrived at the office. Hazelrigg was more upset with what I was saying than with what I had done.

A few explanations:

I was looking for some clue as to what holds a family together.

I was looking to ease my nearly paranoid fear of something else going wrong around me. This, because I was tipsy, upset, and tired. So I wasn't responsible for what I was doing.

I was looking for money, like Monica said.

I wasn't looking for anything.

CHAPTER TWENTY-EIGHT

I gave notice on July 6th. If Pruitt wanted me to, I would work on my regular schedule until the twentieth in order to train my replacement. Since I assumed it would be Mike Strummer, the three or four weeks would be sufficient.

Pruitt's response was to tear up my letter of resignation. He let it flutter to the floor.

"There's no need for this, Howser," he grumbled. "You made a mistake, that's all."

"It's more than that. I was wrong."

"You've worked for me more than five years. I've watched you carefully, I'm sure you know that, and I think you're in the right place here. You can't just float on away."

"It's funny you should use that expression. Just this week, I thought of my life as a balloon that I was losing hold of."

"That's sheer nonsense." He didn't look as convinced as he sounded. "Don't let this silly episode ruin what you've built for yourself."

"Mr. Pruitt, I haven't built anything for myself. In the past two weeks, I've recognized that. My life isn't a balloon, it's more like a pile of materials thrown together whichever way they landed. There's no mortar, just bricks, and nothing but chance is holding it together."

He stared at me for a long time. I remember thinking that I was as astonished by what I'd said as he seemed to be. I hadn't known that's what I thought.

"Then you won't reconsider?"

"I'm gone."

"Well, I tried. That Strummer kid sure isn't ready to take over Pilgrim's Harbor full time."

"Ready doesn't have much to do with anything."

***

I'm in a motel room a good 500 miles due east of Pilgrim's Harbor. It took the Pinto two full days to get this far and I doubt she's going to see the Mississippi next week.

There's enough cash on hand to cover a decent pre-owned with 70,000 or 80,000 on it. I'll see if I can find one; that ought to use up a couple of days, while I get my plans worked out.

Finfer was my first thought. Go hit the campaign trail for a few months. But that was ridiculous. He didn't really have a place for me. Besides, there was Cindy and Jay Ladue.

I'd go home for a while, but there's obvious limitations to that option. Where might home be, Mr. Howser?

So I guess I'll travel for a while. That's what people always told me to do and, for sure, this is the right season for it.

It's strange to pull off the Interstate at the end of the day and start looking for a motel. I pull up and right away my eye finds all sorts of things wrong. It's not easy keeping a place up.

This one badly needs painting. The doors are about as secure as a child's piggy bank. The bedding smells like old milk.

The innkeeper frowned when I tried to strike up a conversation. I didn't really mind. Maybe he's had a bad month, too.

DISCARD

46925020